# TECHNICALLY, YOU STARTED IT

# LANA WOOD JOHNSON

WITHDRAWN

# TECHNICALLY,

## YOU

## STARTED

IT

Scholastic Press / New York

Library of Congress Cataloging-in-Publication Data
Names: Johnson, Lana Wood, author.
Title: Technically, you started it / Lana Wood Johnson.
Description: First edition. | New York: Scholastic Press, 2019. | Summary: In Haley's high school there are two boys named Martin Nathaniel Munroe II (cousins), and one of them has started a text conversation with her, which becomes an all-consuming exchange between two people who see themselves as outsiders. The only trouble is that Haley really doesn't know which Martin she is talking to, and actually meeting face-to-face may lead to an epic meltdown.
Identifiers: LCCN 2018044096 | ISBN 9781338335460
Subjects: LCSH: Text messaging (Cell phone systems)—Juvenile fiction. | High school students—Juvenile fiction. | Interpersonal relations—Juvenile fiction. | Communication—Psychological aspects—Juvenile fiction. | Dating (Social customs)—Juvenile fiction. | Young adult fiction. | CYAC: Text messaging (Cell phone systems)—Fiction. | High schools—Fiction. | Schools—Fiction. | Interpersonal relations—Fiction. | Communication—Fiction. | Dating (Social customs)—Fiction. | Classification: LCC PZ7.1.J6285 Te 2019 | DDC 813.6 [Fic]—dc23

10 9 8 7 6 5 4 3 2 1          19 20 21 22 23

Printed in the U.S.A. at Berryville Graphics in Berryville, Virginia    37
First edition, July 2019

Book design by Baily Crawford

For Michael,
whose Jetta is not crappy

&

for Monica,
whose Jetta kinda was

# FRIDAY, MAY 6
## 8:32 p.m.

Is this Haley Hancock from Mrs. James's US History class?

Yeah.

Who's this?

Which essay question did you pick on the AP test earlier?

Martin Nathaniel Munroe II

Which one? You're both in my US History class.

The good one.

Which question did you choose?

Articles of Confederation . . . right?

No, I picked Watergate.

???

I like Nixon better.

No one likes Nixon better.

His wife does.

Did.

Whatever.

Why does it matter?

Because I bet my cousin that everyone picked the same question.

Thanks to you I lost.

Sorry.

Don't be.

You get the pleasure of proving me wrong.

Only worth it if you're the other Martin.

Wait . . .

You mean I'm the ONLY one in the WHOLE class who picked the Nixon question?

Sure . . .

Rub it in.

You've managed to escape the misery that is a group project.

This is ridiculous! What kind of teacher assigns research projects off the AP test anyway?

Why can't she just let us watch documentaries like in Euro last year?

You're going to get the best grade in the class!

You won't sound like the world's worst morning news anchor as we pass to our teammates during the speech.

I forgot about the speech!

Why did I pick that question?

I don't get why you're freaking out

This is a good thing!

This is the worst thing ever! In a group I have to speak for one minute tops, not five whole minutes.

I'd rather walk over hot coals backward.

I'd give anything to have a solo topic.

Hold on a second. How did you get my number?

Jack . . .

Oh.

Thanks for not having him text me.

Wanted an answer.

So, did you need anything else?

Guess not.

Sorry I disappointed you on your bet or whatever.

I'll just hold it against you forever.

Spoken like a true Martin.

## WEDNESDAY, MAY 11
### 12:25 p.m.

> I am going to need you to pick me up. I can't get the car.

Unexpectedly forward of you, Haley from Mrs. James's US History class.

> Crap, you're not Dylan.

> Whose number is this?

M

> Who?

Martin

From US History

And English.

We've gone to school together since sixth grade.

I texted you last week about the AP questions?

I'm the one who told you you're the only one not at risk of spending the next three weeks analyzing Shays's Rebellion???

Didn't you save my number?

> No, sorry.

> Wrong number.

> Obviously.

I'm hurt.

Didn't you at least notice the message history??

Still there?

No. Sorry, was texting Dylan.

I didn't see the history when I started the message.

I COULD be Dylan if you really needed me to.

Not sure I'm dressed for it.

My mother refuses to purchase flannel in those quantities.

Wait . . . aren't you in German? Why are you texting?

I'm not.

I mean, I am.

In German.

Stop texting me.

Only if you text me in German.

Geh weg, Scheisskopf!

I know what that means

I read Catch-22.

STOP.

I'm not a text service.

That doesn't work on me.

Are you ignoring me?

Really???

You can't turn your phone off

You're waiting for your best friend's ex-boyfriend to answer.

OMG, would you stop?

I knew it!

You're going to get me detention.

Fine . . . I'll leave you alone

Scheisskopf.

**7:45 p.m.**

You're the Scheisskopf, not me.

So you ARE still talking to me

Yes.

No.

I don't know.

Frau was making me conjugate.

Then I had to do something with Dylan after school.

Between which we had class together and YOU said nothing to ME.

Not like you said anything to me either.

I don't know why I'm even texting you now.

But you're still the Scheisskopf.

Which means . . . due to circumstances beyond our control

We're both talking and not talking to each other

And we're both Scheisskopfs?

Pretty much.

## THURSDAY, MAY 12
### 6:13 p.m.

I can't take it anymore.

Why were you texting Dylan?

What?

I know for a fact he and Lexi had a huge fight at prom.

I was there.

So why were you texting him in the middle of German?

And where'd you go with him after school?

Those are kind of personal questions.

They are???

### 8:35 p.m.

How about if I swap a secret?

It's killing you, isn't it?

Maybe.

Now I really shouldn't tell you.

Come on.

There has to be something about me you want to know.

Not especially.

Nothing at all?

Okay, maybe one thing.

???

Why are you both named Martin?

It's our name.

Yes, but why did BOTH your parents name you Martin Nathaniel Munroe II?

They named us after our grandfather.

Duh, really? You were named after the financial genius Martin N. Munroe?

Come on. Who doesn't know that?!

I want to know why the EXACT same thing.

That IS personal.

Maybe we should start with something easier.

Like?

Like why do you always use complete sentences?

What?

You capitalize

Punctuate everything

You even use proper grammar.

Technically, you started it. You had a sentence with subject-verb agreement. Plus, I never quite got skimping on that stuff.

You sound like Ms. Ferguson.

Because Ms. Ferguson is the best English teacher ever!

Don't make me pull out a fifty-cent word on you as punishment.

I'd like to see you try.

Maybe if you're good.

Oh my

I should ask you personal questions more often.

What's that supposed to mean?

Is that your personal question?

No. I think I can figure it out.

Plus, rhetorical questions don't count.

Who made that rule???

I did. Just now.

Fine . . . Rhetorical questions don't count.

What's your question?

Still there???

Shhh! I'm thinking!

You're really not curious about me at all?

I don't know.

I haven't thought about it before.

We've known each other since sixth grade.

Yeah, and?

I'm interesting!

I mean, if you say so.

Ouch!

Okay, fine. Do you have any pets?

My mother has a cat and a dog.

Do you like the cat better?

Not especially.

Why?

You listed the cat first.

Maybe I'm too afraid of her not to give her precedence?

No bonus points for fifty-cent words!

Why are you afraid of the cat?

She's plotting against me.

Pretty sure I'm the first one she'd eat in an apocalypse.

Why? What'd you do to her?

Nothing recently.

But you did do something.

When I was little I MAY have tried to carry her around by her tail.

I'd hate you too!

Good thing you don't have a tail.

What about the dog? Does the dog hate you?

That seems like another personal question.

They're related. Not the same.

Pretty sure it's AT LEAST a second question.

I think this should earn me an extra.

Ugh. Fine. You successfully have me curious.

What does the dog think about you? (+1 personal question)

As a fellow victim of the cat's marauding terror . . . the dog loves me.

He's practically asleep on top of me right now.

Sleeping on you?

Wait . . . now I have you curious?

Not that curious.

Thought I had another question.

No, two is enough.

Two isn't nearly enough.

What's THAT supposed to mean?

I find YOU very interesting.

I'm not even a little bit interesting.

On the contrary.

Given their choice of topics, everyone else would have picked the Watergate break-in for their final paper.

You picked impeachment.

Totally interesting.

And yet you've never asked me a single question in five years. Not interesting.

Now you're a mystery

Wrapped in an enigma

Wrapped in bacon

And fried at 350 degrees until golden brown.

Mmmmmmmmmmmmmmmm, bacon.

You like bacon!

Who doesn't like bacon?

Vegetarians

Actually, I read a study that vegetarians are more likely to break their practice for bacon than any other meat product.

Interesting

And odd.

I thought so too.

Where did you read this?

I don't remember.

My news feed?

That's where I read most things.

Your news feed?

Yeah. Wait, you've asked like three questions.

Not exactly personal ones

They're about vegetarians eating bacon.

Bacon is always personal.

Plus, I told you about my news feed. That's about as personal as it gets.

So you're fond of your news feed?

Yeah. I learn more from it than any day at school ever.

Like???

Like, did you know that acetaminophen can help you stave off existential dread?

Existential dread?

You know, the fear of the future and the meaning of life and all that stuff.

You mean, "Who am I really and will what I do ever be enough?"

How do they test something like that?

THAT'S THE BEST PART!

They made people watch David Lynch movies.

Dune?

No. Something about people in rabbit heads. It's on YouTube. I tried to watch it once.

Dune would make a terrible test.

It's too much fun to watch.

Not the director's cut. It's like twelve hours.

You've seen Dune?

Read it too.

My parents are kinda übernerds.

There's very little I don't know about Dune or any other sci-fi property.

So what you're saying is . . .

Acetaminophen is some kind of Bene Gesserit fear destroyer?

Not all fears. Just existential dread.

Still kind of cool.

And we'd never learn that in AP Bio.

We really wouldn't.

Except I never took AP Bio.

That's right. You were smarter than I was.

How is taking Marine Biology rather than AP Bio smarter?

Oh, wait, I forgot. You're a boy.

AP Bio would not have been a misery because they teach it to your learning style.

You forgot I was a boy?

For a second.

You forgot I was a boy

For a second.

Also what do you mean "my learning style"?

The high school teaching approach for math and sciences favors socialized male behavior and learning styles.

Where'd you hear that?

News feed.

So, what?

You're just giving up???

No, I'm just choosing not to be bothered about my scores until college.

Though I've been doing math online.

Way less judgement from computer programs.

For now.

Yeah, for now.

But sometimes I feel like those quiz timers are laughing at me.

I'll answer your question.

What question did I ask?

Oh. That thing about your name? No, you don't have to.

I just thought it was a joke no one knew. I didn't realize it was that big of a deal.

It's not.

Just sort of . . .

Weird?

Embarrassing.

We've established you know who our grandfather is.

You mean the man single-handedly funding most of the advances in science and technology?

Yes, everyone on the planet knows who your grampa is.

Right.

My father is the oldest

II's father has always been more involved in our grandfather's businesses.

Both our mothers got pregnant at the same time.

As with everything

It became a contest

Because it ALWAYS becomes a contest with them.

Thus . . . both named after our grandfather.

That's why you're both only "the second"?

Grandmother would NEVER name a child after her husband.

So no juniors.

There's only a couple days between us.

My father CLAIMS he left a voicemail, but II was a complicated birth so they never got it.

So what you're saying is—you ended up with exactly the same names because of sibling rivalry?

If you tell anyone . . . I may have to . . .

I don't know but it'll be impressive.

Why would I tell anyone?

Gossip

Attention

Some people think they can sell this stuff.

Especially after my aunt started dating like half of Hollywood.

I can't imagine my aunts ever being in a tabloid.

That's all just so weird!

???

That people would sell your personal stories.

That anyone would pay money for them.

Not MY personal stories

Stories about my grandfather

And my aunt

And any of her boyfriends.

Yeah, no, I get that.

You do?

Yeah. Well, a little.

People freak out when he says he likes something.

I read an article once about an influx of cash in the fabric industry because he wore a special golf shirt.

On your news feed?

Yeah.

I mean, it's not like I'm stalking you guys or anything.

Kind of can't avoid him.

Funny thing is . . . he doesn't even golf.

That IS funny.

Usually I see him because the companies he invests in are really forward thinking.

He's ridiculously smart.

I'd be lucky if I end up half as smart.

You're in all advanced classes.

Not the same

He just gets things.

He's old.

He knows stuff.

My parents are old too.

Sometimes I wonder about them.

Ha, yeah, my grandparents are ancient, and I definitely wonder about them.

No financial geniuses who can shift whole markets?

No, they're more complicated.

Pretty much everything about my family is.

ALL families are complicated

Yeah, but we aren't Forbes and People complicated.

We're more Dr. Phil complicated.

Now THAT'S interesting.

Nope.

That's enough personal stuff tonight. I have to go to bed.

It's only 9:30 and you haven't answered my question.

I have to have my phone plugged in downstairs and be in my bed at 9:30.

I'm pushing it as it is.

Your parents keep you from your phone?

Yeah, it's better for sleep.

Meaning anything I type after this your mother could see?

Or my dad, yeah.

Interesting.

I shouldn't have told you that.

You REALLY shouldn't have.

Good night, Haley from Mrs. James's US History class.

Whatever.

Lexi and Dylan are back together

She seems to be wearing some kind of necklace

Rumor has it . . . almost a hundred roses were shoved in her locker.

But you wouldn't have anything to do with that.

Would you?

## 12:45 p.m.

You haven't blocked me, have you?

I know you saved my number this time.

Right?

Say ja if you're alive . . . nein if you've blocked me.

## 3:45 p.m.

I was in class.

You could have answered "in class."

You could have asked there too.

I could have

You seemed busy.

What? With Sarah? She was just freaking out because she wasn't in on it.

Lexi's romantic surprise?

Yeah, Dylan asked me for help because he REALLY screwed up this time.

Was she refusing to play Courtney to his Kurt?

Geez, could you be more of a snob?

Sorry

I AM interested.

Why? Were you hoping to get back with Lexi first?

That was what . . .

Seventh grade?

I thought it was later than that, ninth maybe?

Whatever.

Answer is definitely still no.

So why ARE you talking to me?

I wanted to know if you had anything to do with Lexi and Dylan getting back together.

Which you don't even really care about.

Don't I?

Maybe

But you owe me an answer.

You mean from last night?

I told you about my family . . .

YOU didn't tell me why you were secretly texting your friend's ex.

Which is something YOU'D never do.

Jack GAVE me your number.

Ugh.

You DID date him.

I went out with Jack.

It's not the same.

And we don't talk about that.

We don't?

How's your research coming? Have you found any sources yet?

Or are you letting your cousin do all your work?

Seriously, though, how'd you both end up in the same group?

Are you mad at me?

What?

No. I'm just confused.

???

You . . . texting me.

Like the first time it made sense. But after that . . .

You texted me back.

And that was a mistake. But I mean after that.

Never mind.

We can talk about the research paper instead.

Finish explaining why out of all the subtopics you picked impeachment over the break-in.

Are you kidding me?

It's a valid question!

You'd pick a botched break-in over the ONE TIME in history Congress actually managed to remove the president from office?

I mean, yeah, he did it himself, but in a you-can't-fire-me-I-quit kinda way.

I thought you were smart.

The break-in has way more drama.

More drama?!?

What is more dramatic than the Supreme Court ruling AGAINST the sitting president?

What's more dramatic than the president actually being brought up on FELONY charges by the legislature?

When you put it that way . . .

G. Gordon Liddy hanging out in a HoJo's does sound a little pedestrian.

Doesn't it?

Plus, you're one to talk. How are you guys coming along on admitting states to the confederation?

Sure . . . rub it in.

But, seriously, there's no way you, your cousin, Chloe, AND Sarah ended up together by chance.

I think it was rigged.

Not by me!

No, by Sarah if anyone.

???

Unlike you, she's a big fan of group work when it's basically the perfect group.

Look at you being all mysterious again.

I'm not being mysterious.

I'm researching possible sources for my bibliography.

Mysterious AND responsible?

Intriguing.

You haven't started yet?

The bibliographies aren't due until Tuesday.

How can you complain about anyone else not pulling their weight if you're not even going to do the research properly?

I have four days!

And you can start now!

I've got a raid tonight!

Oh, I guess you can start tomorrow.

You know what raiding is?

I'm not in a guild or anything, but we do Karazhan sometimes for family night.

Are you a tank or DPS?

Healer

You've got to be kidding me.

Healers are the best.

Not that.

Why is every guy I know a healer?

You know OTHER healers?

My dad is basically a real-life Paladin. He's always helping people and doing good and stuff.

That's like the only character type he plays.

My uncle is a healer too. But he does it for the challenge, not the goodness.

Half the time of family raids is spent convincing someone to re-spec tank.

What do you play?

Hunter, like my mom . . . all about doing the most damage per second.

When I play, that is. I haven't done much online in the last year or so.

We're more into board games lately, which is what we're doing tonight.

I'm seeing you in a whole new light, Haley from Mrs. James's US History class.

Yeah, well. This is what happens when you actually talk to people.

???

Look, I gotta go, I'm in charge of the snicky-snacks.

Mustn't keep a girl from her "snicky-snacks."

You're right. Otherwise my dad will make a vegetable tray.

Healthy "snicky-snacks"???

Definitely can't have that.

Anyway . . . good luck keeping ungrateful tanks alive.

Good luck snacking or whatever.

## SATURDAY, MAY 14
### 10:27 a.m.

What do you know about lawn mowers?

Little to nothing . . . why?

Mine won't start.

That's unfortunate.

I thought maybe your news feed would know something about them.

My news feed has better things to worry about than internal combustion engines.

Don't you have people who mow your lawn for you?

My grandfather has people.

My father has an association.

My mother has me

And this archaic lawn mower that refuses to start.

When is the last time it started?

Sometime last fall.

And did you drain the gasoline?

Why would I do that?

Well, that's your problem.

You're gonna need to drain the gasoline, get new gas, and maybe clean your spark plugs or whatever.

I thought you said you knew little to nothing about lawn mowers.

I don't. My dad does. He also likes to complain about people who don't take care of theirs.

AND he likes to tell us what a good job he does in comparison.

Your father sounds like a rather clever person.

I see where you get it.

I mean, I guess. Mostly he does it to impress my mom.

Your mother is impressed by his mechanical prowess?

Mom is even more clever than he is.

Dad likes to prove he's up to the task of conversing with her.

THAT'S where you get it from

I'll have to remember that trick.

Don't you have a lawn mower to fix?

And clever things to come up with.

Until next time.

Thanks for your help yesterday.

Did you get it figured out?

Sort of . . .

Sort of?

The lawn got mowed.

But you didn't fix the mower?

A new mower was purchased.

So you failed.

I was not given the opportunity to fail!!!!!

Right.

Lack of faith. I get it.

My mother's boyfriend purchased a new one.

Just on a whim?

Not exactly.

Did he take pity on you?

Not exactly.

Kindness of his heart?

Would you believe bribery???

He was bribing you with a mower?

When you say it like that it sounds weird.

It is weird.

Please say it was at least a riding mower.

Now taking up a good chunk of the garage stall.

I have to park on the street.

This seems impractical.

Doesn't it?

Well, I'm glad your lawn got mowed.

And I'm glad you figured it out because my dad says it was probably the carburetor, not the spark plugs, and that sounds WAY more complicated.

That makes me feel better.

I'm still working on coming up with something clever.

You've managed odd.

So that's at least something.

Is it?

Odd I can work with.

## MONDAY, MAY 16
### 5:45 p.m.

Did you know part of Tennessee originally wanted to join the confederation as the state of Frankland?

That's . . . nice?

Did you want points for a fact about pre-constitutional America I didn't know or for finally doing your homework?

Going for clever but if I hit the trifecta . . . I'm OK with that.

So is that what your part of the speech will be? Frankland?

No.

Just digging through some of the resources.

Did you know there were three states that petitioned to join the confederation?

No, but I'm not surprised.

Just not the one everyone seemed to WANT to join.

Let me guess: Canada?

Quebec

Technically.

Good, no one wants them anyway.

I guess they were holding out for a better deal.

Like I should have for this group.

Don't blame Sarah or Chloe for your bad choices. You had your chance to pick Nixon with me and failed.

Don't I know it.

But this is making up for it.

How?

Did you know Kentucky almost joined but New Hampshire totally undermined them by ratifying the Constitution before they got anywhere?

I don't know if the Constitution could count as undermining.

I mean on a state level.

I guess there was plenty of undermining of native people and slaves in there.

And women in general.

Too bad that question wasn't on the test or we could tackle THAT instead.

But what about you?

Have you found anything good?

Just ludicrous excuses for destroying evidence.

I honestly don't know if they thought the American people were that stupid or if they were just desperate.

Probably a little of both.

Have you decided what your visual aid is going to be?

Still working on it.

I want to do something a bit more than just a PowerPoint, but I don't know what yet.

Sarah has this whole Northwest Territory animation she wants to do, so we're going to get together next week and figure it out.

How about you?

Clearly not a Northwest Territory animation.

Is your group communicating at all?

We're doing our best despite not picking Mrs. James's favorite topic.

What was she talking about today?

That thing about the senate?

The Senate Select Committee on Presidential Campaign Activities. We covered it in class.

And there's the reason I didn't pick that question on the AP test.

Yeah, well, it doesn't help me any.

That was the "What does the president know and when did he know it?" stuff.

Mine's WAY after that. When they figured out he was definitely up to enough they couldn't ignore.

There's a whole progression.

It's kind of fun.

You should do a timeline.

Like, "What DID the president know and when did he know it?"

Maybe more like, "What did we figure out about the president and when did we figure it out?"

Doesn't have the same ring to it.

What about you?

Are you just going to make an ode to Canada?

When Sarah's making us a whole animation???

I don't know if Canada's interesting enough.

I need something flashier.

This is a visual aid for one-quarter of a five-minute speech, not a Broadway show.

Not flashy then.

I mean, you could use some sparkle transitions if you really want to, but that would only work if Nevada had been trying to join.

Kentucky deserves better than that.

I could have Vermont appear as if from nowhere and wipe Frankland off the map.

You could have an anthropomorphized Constitution chasing Kentucky away.

You are OFFICIALLY not helping.

Not in my interest to help.

But you're going to help Sarah?

It's always in my best interest to help her.

You guys are that good of friends?

Since forever.

What about you? You going to help your cousin?

He doesn't need it.

He needs all the help he can get.

Starting to get the feeling you don't like him very much.

Wow, you are quick.

Look, I have to go, my dad's calling me.

???

Good luck with your states that had to wait to join the Union rather than the confederation.

Good luck with your treason.

It was abuse of power.

???

Not treason. He was never accused of treason.

Abuse of power, obstruction of justice, and contempt of Congress.

They tried to get him on tax evasion, but it failed.

Why does EVERYONE go down on tax evasion?

Well, if you're going to be bad, be all the way bad and not file your taxes.

My grandfather is a stickler for taxes.

Well, someone in your family has to be a stickler for something.

Did I do something?

Not you.

That cousin of yours.

And I'M being punished????

Figures.

What'd he do this time?

Dumped his girlfriend a week after prom.

II hasn't had a date in the week and a half since prom, let alone a girlfriend to break up with.

We went with Josie and Chloe for a group hangout thing.

I don't remember specifying anyone was anyone else's date.

We even met at the restaurant.

That's not the way they saw it.

Chloe's basically been in tears all week.

That sucks.

She seemed fine today.

Well, yeah.

You guys are in a group with him. She's not going to give him the satisfaction.

She and I talked after class and she didn't say anything.

Of course she wouldn't say anything to you, you're practically the same person.

We are NOT the same person.

Well, whatever.

So that's why you weren't talking to me?

What?

You didn't bother correcting me for three days?

Clearly this has been bothering you.

Well, maybe a little.

That and I didn't see your last message.

I see.

I'm not my cousin.

What?

We're different people.

Me and Jack too.

We spend a lot of time together but we're not all the same.

I know that.

I realize things didn't end well with you and Jack.

Why are you bringing that up? It was practically nothing.

It didn't seem like nothing.

We sat next to each other at one movie and shared a booth at like three restaurants.

It wasn't some torrid love affair.

We were barely alone.

Didn't you guys talk like every day?

I mean, yeah, we texted a few times.

But I think I've texted you more at this point than I did him.

Huh.

What?

Nothing

Just huh.

That seems like more than just huh.

He may see things a little differently

How could he see things differently? We barely held hands.

You DID hold hands.

He was helping me out of the car.

Which in itself was weird.

So you have NO IDEA he still likes you?

WHAT?

No.

You're being ridiculous.

The entire school knows he likes you.

He asked you to prom.

He did not. No one asked me to prom.

Jack made a terrible joke about prom at me.

Not the same thing.

He what?

We went out for like half a second last summer thanks to Lexi and Sarah's meddling. No way he still likes me. You're being dramatic.

I think I know him a bit better than you do.

Didn't he have some epic date anyway?

You mean like the date II supposedly had with Chloe?

I don't know. I don't really pay attention.

Unless they're crying?

And blocking the sink. Yeah.

She was blocking the sink???

Most overly dramatic conversations block the sink.

I guess he said something today and set Chloe off again.

Sarah managed to get the whole story out of her, and there was a lot of commiserating.

Well . . . that explains the dramatics.

What's that supposed to mean?

Just that Sarah tends to take things a bit further than they need to go.

She just REALLY likes the people she likes.

In her own Sarah way.

Oh, right, I guess you had front-row seats for one of Sarah's most epic romances.

You could say that.

So are you not mad at me now?

I don't know.

Are you and your friends going to do a better job of defining your relationships going forward?

I'll do my best

Can't speak for II or Jack.

I guess that's all I can hope for, really.

Wouldn't want to further inconvenience you and your handwashing.

Handwashing is important! It reduces the spread of germs.

Before the 1850s we didn't realize how important it was and everyone died of typhus.

You mean typhoid?

Whatever.

I refuse to die of typhus for your love life.

That's all I ask.

I can at least guarantee that much.

## SUNDAY, MAY 22
### 9:03 p.m.

I just noticed you never use gifs.

Or emojis.

### 9:14 p.m.

Are you even there?

I never saw the point of gifs.

Mom says it's genetic.

Your mother knows what a gif is?

Yes. Doesn't yours?

My mother barely knows Facebook exists.

My mom's been on the internet since before Google.

Actually, before browsers.

I told you I was raised nerd.

How can you not see the point of gifs?

They're equal parts hilarious and clever.

Well, they're expensive (bandwidth- and processor-wise) and words are better than pictures.

You don't LIKE pictures?

I like looking at pictures.

I just don't communicate in pictures. I communicate in words.

Interesting.

Even my great-grandma spelled everything after she got dementia.

You knew your great-grandmother?

Yeah. Women in my family live forever.

My mom knew her great-great-grandma.

That's kind of cool.

She was the one who migrated from Germany. On her own . . . at fourteen.

How do you know that?

Another thing I get from my mom.

Technology, genealogy, and a general indifference to visuals.

I guess they're all just data structures or something.

She'd be happy to explain that as much as my dad would lawn mowers.

What about you?

What do you like to explain?

Whatcha got?

What do you actually like to talk about?

Like when you and Lexi and Sarah have sleepovers or whatever.

Do you want to know what I like to talk about or what we talk about at sleepovers?

There's a difference?

A big one.

Now I'm intrigued.

But knowing them . . . I want to know what you like to talk about.

It's kinda weird.

Weirder than your mother's boyfriend bribing you with lawn equipment?

Okay, not that weird.

I don't really watch television-television.

Are you one of those no TV families?

More like we don't have cable. My mom and I watch mostly Korean TV.

And my dad watches Canadian blacksmithing videos on YouTube.

Korean TV? Where does that even come from?

Korea.

But I get it on the internet.

Where???

Uhm, everywhere? I guarantee you wherever you get your internet TV there's dramas.

No way.

Search. Prove me wrong.

Holy crap.

You're right!

It's SO happy!

That's just the intro.

Whatever you just played, I guarantee you it gets sad at some point!

Why do you seem excited???

OMG, the sad is the best part. Well, not too sad.

Not tragedy porn.

I don't watch those.

Tragedy porn?

Yeah, the girl has a brain tumor or he has cancer or they're siblings. And they meet, fall in love, and die.

Siblings???

Yeah, I don't watch those.

I WAS going to reevaluate everything I knew about you.

You don't know that much about me.

I know MORE now.

You read A LOT of news

Have a strange obsession with Nixon

Are an ardent hand washer

Loyal to friends even when it seems like you're not.

And now . . .

Watches East Asian television.

I watch KOREAN television.

There's a difference.

There's a difference among East Asian television shows?

Well, Asia IS the largest, most populated continent. We're talking about OVER A BILLION people in East Asia alone. OF COURSE their entertainment varies widely.

Taiwanese is too slapstick. Japanese is too . . . not for me.

You don't like Japanese television?

Not even anime???

You like anime?

Some.

What? Giant fighting robots?

And magic girls!!!

Male gaze much?

I'm beginning to see you in a totally new light, Haley from Mrs. James's US History class.

Whatever.

I'm going to go watch something.

Upon further reflection . . .

In our conversation last night I MAY have come across both a little racist and sexist.

I apologize if I offended you.

Upon further further reflection . . .

My apology MAY have been as offensive as the original statement.

I apologize for being insensitive.

Wow, no wonder you're in all advanced classes.

I get there eventually.

Persistent like a bull.

Bulls are more immovable than persistent.

You're persistent like a terrier.

Less noble

But I'll take it!

As long as you know to be sorry.

But I didn't ignore you for that reason. I was out last night.

On a school night?

Yeah, Lexi and I went to Sarah's to work on our visual presentations.

Lexi offered to help because she's kind of a wiz with PowerPoint.

Do you now have a three-dimensional timeline of the Nixon impeachment?

Uh, no. Chloe was there because she had this really great idea for Sarah's animation.

It took a while, but we actually got the lapping waves of Lake of the Woods glistening in the sun.

You AND Lexi spent the WHOLE time at Sarah's working on OUR group's project BECAUSE of Chloe?

Mine's gonna be pretty easy.

It just needs a timeline.

I thought you wanted something more dramatic.

My speech is dramatic enough.

I don't need flash, I've got the truth on my side.

Just like Senator Baker had the tapes.

You didn't need to work on my group's homework when you're the one who doesn't have any help.

It wasn't a big deal. I don't even really know what I want to do.

Sarah has to keep up with the three of you.

I just have to finish mine.

Is that why you wanted to be in a group?

So you didn't have to come up with everything on your own?

I did, but now I'm too afraid I'd wind up like you guys . . . fighting all the time.

Which reminds me! I have something you can do if you want to make up for being an insensitive jerk.

I didn't say insensitive jerk.

No, I did.

OK.

I was an insensitive jerk.

So, if you want to make it up to me, tell me what you were arguing about.

What who was arguing about?

During your group planning today.

When things got dramatic.

We weren't talking about you if that's what you were wondering.

Really? Because evil-Martin was glaring at me after whatever Chloe said that was so funny.

???

Right before he started yelling at her?

My COUSIN was glaring at you today?

Well, not glaring AT me, but glaring in my direction.

And then yelled at Chloe?

Yeah, what set him off? It must have been hilarious based on your and Sarah's reaction.

I laughed at Chloe and my cousin got mad?

Yeah, it was bizarre.

Do you not remember this?

I just want to be clear:

The Martin you hate didn't laugh with Sarah but was upset by what Chloe said?

Hate is kind of a strong term.

Evil's kind of a strong term.

Not really.

Seems to fit him.

It does?

We're still talking about the Martin who got mad at Chloe?

He's just so convinced he's god's gift.

Look

I have to go.

My mother's calling me.

Oh, okay.

So, I think I owe you an apology.

I'm sorry for saying terrible, senseless things about your cousin.

It occurs to me I don't really know him except secondhand and so, probably, I have let my judgemental nature get the better of me.

It's only . . .

The way he treated Sarah was irresponsible, and I haven't seen much lately that would improve my opinion of him.

**8:15 p.m.**

Sarah was eighth grade.

And?

We're nearly seniors.

Not yet.

Still.

You weren't there when he broke her heart.

And I know he makes like every girl that looks at him cry, but she cried the worst.

Again I say . . . It was eighth grade!

We were what???

Thirteen?????

And she's my best friend.

It wasn't right.

Nothing about it was right

But it was four years ago.

Yeah. Well. I guess.

Can't believe you've been mad that long

Even she's not still mad.

She wasn't.

???

Chloe's situation brought it all back.

They've been bonding over it or something.

I explained that to you

It was a misunderstanding.

It seems to happen to him a lot.

Not like you haven't done the same thing.

What?

MY best friend?

Jack?

I didn't even want to go out with him in the first place.

I thought I explained THAT to YOU.

Doesn't mean he's any less hurt.

I'm sorry. I still think you're being ridiculous, but if I did hurt him, it wasn't what I wanted.

None of this was remotely what I wanted.

You and me both

But there's one thing I really want to know

What's that?

Obviously you're mad about both Sarah and Chloe

Not mad. Just not ready to let go of the grudge.

Fine

You're still grudge-y.

Why are you still talking to me?

Why? Because you and your cousin are like joined at the hip?

To the point you think we're the same person

Yes.

Honestly?

I don't know.

You don't know why you're willing to talk to one Martin and not the other?

Oh.

That.

Are you still there?

This is the first time I really felt like I was talking to someone.

???

I know it must sound strange.

I talk to people all the time. I even have a couple of friends.

Har, har.

But this is different?

Ugh, that sounds so dorky.

Don't you have to go soon?

Yeah, in like two minutes.

You're not mad at me still?

I was more confused than mad.

Are you still confused?

No

Yeah.

OK very.

I won't bother you anymore.

You're not bothering me.

Yeah, but . . .

But???

I was harsh.

And I'm still grudge-y.

But I can't expect you to just be okay with this when I'm not.

Even though you're right, Sarah was eighth grade.

See!

Yeah. I won't make you talk to me.

I know how I can be.

Not that

This just isn't going the way I thought.

Okay, well, I have to go now anyway.

So I guess you'll have plenty of time to think.

Good night, only Haley in Mrs. James's US History class.

Good night, one of two Martins in Mrs. James's US History class.

## SUNDAY, MAY 29
### 7:42 a.m.

I think I know how to make this work.

### 11:35 a.m.

How?

### 1:58 p.m.

Sorry I was at church, followed directly by family dinner.

You go to church?

Oh, wait, duh, you guys all go together.

Every Sunday.

Don't you?

No. Never. But Mom tells me about it all the time.

Your mother tells you about church?

Yeah, she went to a super religious church or three growing up.

What's a super religious church?

One where girls can't speak.

I can't see you going to one of those.

Yeah, I can't see my mom going to one either, but that's how she grew up.

My dad didn't. He thinks he was Lutheran, but Mom has to remind him his whole family is Catholic.

That's what I am.

Catholic?

Lutheran.

Oh, the good kind or the kind like my mom went to?

I am SO NOT going to presume which of anything you think is good anymore.

Nah, I'll bet it's the good kind.

Again . . .

Not playing that with you.

I do go to the kind that lets women lead

So it more than likely matches your definition this time.

What were you saying about a solution?

What if I weren't Martin and you weren't Haley?

But we are?

This whole friendship started online.

What if we were

I don't know

Actual internet friends.

You mean like people who never met in person and had no baggage about exes?

Still baggage

But the other person doesn't think they already know all about the baggage.

Hrm.

What do you think?

Let's try it.

I mean, you are kinda interesting to talk to.

And I helped you with your lawn mower.

Yeah

You're better than Google.

NO ONE is better than Google.

OK so I hit a nerve.

I may not be religious, but I do believe in algorithms.

So you're not going to try talking to me in school?

And you're going to keep pretending like you don't know me to anyone else?

You wish I pretended like you knew me.

That doesn't even make sense.

Go with it, internet friend.

Do not call me that.

No one says that.

What should I call you?

I don't know. Just Haley?

All right, Just Haley.

You're incorrigible.

Fifty-cent word! I AM in trouble.

As long as you know it. So, friends?

Friends.

Hi, friend.

Not now.

Busy?

Family stuff.

Good stuff?

Cousins.

I know how that goes.

Not the same.

Talk later.

So you also have cousins.

Yeah, they're all younger, though.

More than a week?

Much . . .

Toddlers.

They're cute, but OMG, so much energy.

Put them down for a nap.

Works on II when he gets fussy.

Ha! Don't you think we all tried?

No, my dad was grilling. They decided there would be no naps while there was still meat.

Mmmm . . . meat.

Also salad.

Meat and salad?

Yeah, my dad makes a mean salad.

And grilled vegetables.

Your family is interesting.

They're kinda normal.

Which is interesting.

Did you need something yesterday?

Maybe some meat

But I didn't know that was an option.

It still is. About half our fridge is meat.

Didn't your family eat it?

You underestimate the amount of meat my father prepares.

Pretty sure he thinks he's supposed to feed half the state.

Your father sounds like good people.

What did you do for Memorial Day?

Hot dogs

Don't you guys have some big thing?

Grandfather's company does.

And you don't have to go?

Isn't this veering close to people who know each other?

Oh.

Right.

Sorry.

Time for stranger questions.

Stranger questions?

Pretend you don't know anything about me at all.

Like an internet person.

Oh.

Like what?

Like what are you doing after school?

Putting the finishing touches on my speech.

You're up first, right?

Yep. First screwup.

Good to get it all out of the way.

You would say that.

How about you?

Somewhere in the middle.

You ready to follow the year's best short-form animation?

More than.

I meant what are you doing after finals?

Next week? Mom made me get a summer job.

People still do that?

Yeah. Well, I do.

Where?

The gas station down the street.

What kind of gas station?

The one with the big mini-mart.

With the good burritos?!

Those things are NOT good.

They're like fifty billion calories.

As I said.

Ew.

What about you?

Not much.

Church baseball league

Lots of video games

Family "vacation"

I guess I KIND OF have a summer job.

Technically an internship.

An internship? So, one of your relatives got you a desk job?

My mother.

Ooh, what does she do?

She works in an architecture firm.

Really?

Surprised?

A little.

Doing what?

Me or her?

You.

Not as cushy or desk-like as you think

I have to run around a lot.

In this case "intern" means "unpaid errand boy."

So, what, you have to get them coffee?

Run plans to sites

Take pictures of things

I barely get to even LOOK at a computer.

No AutoCAD for you?

Of course you know all about
architectural plotting software.

So is that what you want to do?

Architecture?

Yeah.

Not really.

But it's better than working for any of my
other relatives.

Is your mom an architect?

CPA.

Oooh, money.

Makes sense.

There you go making assumptions again.

Oh, right.

Sorry.

So do you want to be in money?

Not really.

I guess I don't have much choice

Money's just not that interesting.

Your relatives seem to disagree.

They're wrong.

So what is interesting?

Don't know yet

Still trying to figure that out.

Do you want to work in gas stations your whole life??

Ha, no.

Clearly.

What DO you want to do?

What do you mean?

Like do you have plans to use your cleverness to change the world?

Well, obviously.

I just don't quite know exactly how yet.

So you're like me.

If you mean totally going to do something big just not the first clue what, then yes. Exactly like you.

Exactly.

Until then . . . burrito slinging?

Ugh, when you put it that way . . .

Probably should have thought that one through better.

Just a bit.

Hey, stranger.

What are you reading?

How did you know I was reading?

I took a shot.

It's an article about earthquake swarms in volcanoes.

Swarms as in bees?

Kinda. It's like baby earthquakes so you don't forget the mountain can blow up and kill you anytime.

I'm glad we live where the world doesn't pull that kind of stuff on us.

You and me both.

Though there's that fault down in Missouri.

Moved the Mississippi?

Made it run backward.

VERY cool.

What were you doing?

Pretending to study.

Pretending?

My only final tomorrow is English . . .

So, you're studying what? All the mistakes you made on English papers this year in the hopes of winning the Grudge Match Spelling Bee?

What mistakes?

I'M going to triumph in the spelling bee tomorrow because I make no mistakes and thus will school all my classmates on theirs.

You wish.

Grudge Match Spelling Bee is the best final.

Because Ms. Ferguson is the best. What other teacher would use the final to win back points we lost on our old assignments?

Oh, wait, this is breaking the rules.

Right. We don't know each other.

So you don't know I'm pretending to study to beat one particular snarky girl in my English class tomorrow so she'll know I'm worthy of speaking to her.

I'd believe that except you have to study and real snarky girls already know how to spelll

I see you also have your auto-correct turned off . . .

Tell me again how you're going to triumph?

Argh! Stupid fingers! That doesn't count!

How about, instead, you explain WHY you're pretending to study for something you have no hope of winning?

There's more trouble in paradise.

Your parents?

Step2's annual review is in.

She's not meeting or exceeding expectations.

Step2?

My second stepmother.

Not as pretty as Step1.

Nor as patient with my father's nonsense.

But neither did they fall in love when still young and innocent like with my mother.

What she IS is richer and smarter than him.

So . . . doomed to failure from the start.

Oh. I didn't realize.

That this is his third marriage

Or that my father has awful taste in women?

I guess either.

Not something we talk about.

This one was one of his investors.

And your mom was his accountant?

High school sweetheart.

Step1 was his partner's assistant . . .

Ouch.

Embarrassing.

Before or after?

My parents' divorce?

After.

Sorry, I shouldn't pry.

It was a long time ago.

Yeah, but it's your family.

I survived the last two.

I'll survive this one.

If he could wait more than a second before getting remarried . . . that'd be something.

Sorry.

My family's just a mess.

No, it's all right. My parents are a lone normal spot in a family of super weird.

My grampa once dated a countess.

???

Not a real countess. An online gaming countess.

I just spit water all over my phone!!!

Yeah, and he's the reasonably okay one on that side.

My dad's side is so average they freak Mom out, but they're still kinda odd.

Odd? Like uneven?

Exactly, normal on the outside, weird family secrets on the inside.

Family secrets???

I can get behind that.

You have family secrets?

One does not grace the pages of Forbes and People without a FEW secrets.

Good point.

So, okay, if it's within the rules . . . what does your grampa really do?

I mean, I know he's famous and rich and his company is freaking huge, and I get that he's a huge investor, but like, what does he DO every day?

No one knows.

That's the thing.

Basically he has a bunch of meetings after which he moves money around.

My grandfather inherited a small country bank from HIS father and turned that into an "investment firm."

Are those scare quotes?

Pretty much.

They at least explain why you went with an architecture internship.

My father wants to prove he can make his own money.

He's got these schemes.

Stuff my grandfather would never invest in.

So he's a risk-taker.

Huge risk-taker.

My dad isn't.

He's like the most boring supernerd ever.

Must be nice.

Some days.

Do your parents argue?

You mean other than about some supremely minute point of trivia?

Other than that.

Nope.

Must be real nice.

Yeah, but . . .

But???

I guess my dad's parents never really argued either, and then all of a sudden they divorced.

There must have been a reason.

Yeah, I guess.

I've lived through 2.5 divorces.

There's always a reason.

You think you're in the middle of another one?

Trust me

I'm a professional.

That sucks.

You get used to it.

If it makes you feel any better, I worry about my parents divorcing all the time.

But they get along and don't argue.

It's not rational.

I kinda worry about everything.

I worry I'm gonna get hit by a bus.

You don't take the bus.

Exactly.

Is this something acetaminophen helps?

Hah!

No.

I take stuff, but it only makes it . . . less.

Less bad?

Less urgent. Less . . . everything I think about.

But you still worry?

A lot.

Is this a diagnosed thing?

Generalized anxiety disorder.

That sounds nicely vague.

It's not. It's really specific. It means I worry about nothing and everything.

Well, no, sometimes I worry about real things.

But that's easier.

How is worrying about real things easier?

At least I know why I'm worrying and sometimes I can even do something about it.

You think it's weird, right?

Not as weird as gaming royalty.

I wonder how many times we have to run through Uldir on mythic before I can call myself a duke.

OMG, I never should have told you that.

But really

It's equally as weird as multiple stepparents by the time you're seventeen.

That's not weird.

In fact, that is kind of normal.

I'm the weird one.

Freak parents who like each other and don't fight.

Who does that?

Kind of weird.

So what about your mom?

What about her?

I mean, has she remarried?

Not yet.

Not yet?

Been dating this one guy for a while.

CHUCK.

The one with the lawn mower?

Is he angry or something?

No

Just . . . boisterous.

But I still worry about her.

Why?

They've been off and on for years.

She's going to be lonely when I leave.

Do you mostly stay at her house?

At this point I go back and forth.

50/50.

Probably 80/20 after the divorce.

Your dad won't want you around?

Opposite. We do more stuff together when he's alone

Which won't be very long.

Total serial monogamist.

He can't be alone for five minutes.

So while he hunts I'll fill the gaps.

How does that even work?

We'll mostly watch movies in his home theater.

No, I mean the serial monogamy.

Well, the serial part. Monogamy is pretty straightforward.

He can't handle the idea of being alone.

But he just finds women to marry him?

Or date him for that matter?

Like, what? Are they hiding under couch cushions or something?

I told you where he's finding them

At work.

I mean, yeah, but . . .

How do you do it?

???

You've dated like three-quarters of our grade and reasonable chunks of all the others.

Where do you get this???

Observation.

You're observing the wrong things.

Plus

It's not like I'm making a commitment to everyone I see a movie with.

We have fun.

There's a difference?

What was the difference with you and Jack?

I should let you go.

You have that test to study for.

Sorry

That was low.

No, just suppertime.

Then I'm going to read the dictionary or something.

Scared now?

As if.

You're petrified.

In your dreams.

We'll see who reigns tomorrow.

Theoretically . . . of course.

Of course.

We're seniors!!!!!

Not really. Not until school starts again.

Plus, we don't have our grades yet.

Like either of us is going to be held back.

You're feeling optimistic.

Not as optimistic as Lexi.

Oh man, did you get the speech?

You mean "We should really stay in touch this summer. It'll be the best of our lives"?

That's the one.

Everyone got the speech.

She was giving it to a freshman at lunch.

Oh, that was probably Dylan's sister.

They've started going shopping together and stuff.

She's not wrong.

I intend for this to be a very good summer.

Just not entirely sure how.

You do?

I already have a new internet friend!

Har, har.

Lexi actually has plans on making sure this "best summer of our lives" works.

There are icebreakers, activities, and hangouts.

What is she??? Senior summer cruise director?

Something like that.

You don't sound excited.

I mean.

I'm not UNexcited.

I think you are.

I don't know.

I just don't really see the point of going out all the time.

Or doing stupid online polls.

???

Bonding exercises.

No trust falls for you?

I would not put it past her.

What does Sarah think?

Sarah, unlike me, thinks it's fabulous.

But Sarah, unlike me, agrees with her new friend Chloe that it's important that we maintain a certain social standing.

I see.

I mean, you all go to church together. Isn't that social enough for all of you?

That's not why we go to church.

Right, but . . .

You're not excited to be a senior

You're not excited for the epic summer your best friend has planned

What ARE you excited for?

I don't know. Time to myself?

Today is not a good day.

I guess.

You should go have fun.

It's an epic "first night of freedom."

I hear there's going to be pizza.

You're not going to hang out?

I was ASSURED it was going to be "amazing."

Unless the hanging out is on my couch, nope.

What about you?

Don't know.

Was going to swing by

But maybe not now.

You should go.

Not much point.

I've infected you.

My ennui.

As contagious as typhus.

I'll leave you to your ennui.

Thanks, I guess.

Just do me a favor

Don't watch any Lynch movies.

Don't want you descending into existential dread.

Oh, good point.

Maybe I should take an acetaminophen just in case.

Or just watch something else.

Don't worry

This IS going to be a good summer.

Don't worry?

HAH.

As if.

## MONDAY, JUNE 6
### 7:45 p.m.

Have you started your job yet?

Yeah, I like JUST got home.

Why? Did you start yours?

Been home for hours.

Cushy office jobs.

It wasn't THAT cushy. Had to run about three billion errands.

Isn't that illegal? Or really expensive on your insurance?

Driving?

Yeah. I was thinking about it and started to think about the crash risks of teen drivers.

You were worrying about me???

What?

No.

I was worrying about being on the road with you.

You were worried I'd get into an accident.

Well, your premiums would go up.

You were worried I'd crash and something would happen to me.

No.

You'll be happy to know that I did not crash once.

Didn't even come close.

That doesn't mean you shouldn't be careful.

Most accidents happen because the driver is overconfident.

You ARE worried about me!

Knew it.

I am not.

Oh, you won't guess who came in today.

I wouldn't know who visited you at your job.

We're complete strangers. Remember?

Oh . . . right.

No

Please tell me about it.

No, never mind, it's just weird.

Weird like . . . gamer princess weird

Or maniac clown weird?

Urgh.

Neither.

Just a kid from one of my classes.

On a scale of gamer princess to maniac clown where does this visitor land?

Way closer to maniac clown.

And why was this maniac clown's visit notable?

Well, to a stranger such as you it wasn't notable at all.

Oh, except he ate one of your precious burritos.

NO!!!!!

THOSE ARE MY BURRITOS!

Oh, whatever. You would never eat one of my burritos.

You never know . . .

I could find my way to your burritos.

I'm QUITE clever.

I guard my burritos well.

Clearly not if you let maniac clowns eat them.

Well, he paid for it.

You think I wouldn't pay for your burritos???

I am SO not going to answer that.

Don't.

I took that metaphor a bit too far.

Back to the clown.

SUCH a good name for him.

To a stranger like you, yes, some clown came in and bought a burrito and left.

The chances of this clown sharing genetic material with you would be absurd. Seeing as you're a complete internet stranger who could be from anywhere.

The chances of this clown having my name would be astronomical?

Yep.

You're right

This is the most boring story ever.

Totally boring. Not of any interest whatsoever.

Do you feel your conversation with this clown went well?

I guess he's working nearby or was in the neighborhood or something.

He threatened to visit again.

No!!!!!

How DARE a paying customer return to your store!?!

What kind of two-bit operation are you running over there in gas station land?

See, I told you, it's a terrible story for a stranger.

If you were someone I knew, it would be a bit more interesting.

Don't know

Kind of like you telling me these tales of legally-purchased-burrito-eating not-quite-maniac clowns.

Ha.

When you put it that way . . .

See, I can be clever if I practice.

So, tell me about your day. Other than not crashing and dying horribly in a mangled wreck.

I KNEW you were worried about me.

I was NOT worried about you.

It's OK

I will accept your worry.

Basically all I do is go around to the job sites with notes and updates and stuff.

One time they had me carry back this mud they found.

Ooh, what kind of mud was it?

Don't know

They were saying something about it being a kind of clay.

Oh man, you should have taken a picture.

Of the mud?

Yeah. Geology is cool. I'll bet they were worried about the footings or something.

How do you know that?

Uh.

You can't laugh.

You wouldn't know if I were laughing or not.

Something you read?

No.

It was a podcast.

Like one of those news article podcasts?

No.

Was it a mud fetishist podcast???

Wouldn't that be a better YouTube channel than a podcast?

Ew! No! It's a geology podcast, okay?

You listen to geology podcasts . . .

I told you, you couldn't laugh.

Do I sound like I'm laughing?

You're laughing. I can tell.

OK I'm laughing a LITTLE.

Why in the world do you listen to geology podcasts?

Where did you even find one?

It's just one podcast.

I was interested in learning more, so I found it.

You know, after the swarm earthquake article.

That was last week!!!

Right. So I went to look for more cool stuff about geology.

In four days you've become a geology podcast groupie?

I AM NOT A GROUPIE!

I just listened to a whole bunch of episodes.

They talked about cool stuff. Not just earthquake swarms.

They were talking about lead and mud and schist.

Did you know that North America has another plate shoved up underneath it?

Tectonic plates?

Yeah. Oh wait. Are you creationist?

No, judgy pants.

Keep telling me all about your geology fetish.

IT'S NOT A FETISH!

Tell me more about your newfound interest in all things geology so that you basically have a PhD in four days.

I don't know that much! I just listened to a few casts is all.

Okay, like twenty.

But it's not a big deal.

Right . . .

But get this. The Pacific coast all the way through the Rockies and then even the Great Plains almost all the way to us has a plate shoved under it.

And some of the earthquake stuff on the West Coast is the last of that plate trying to go under with the rest of it.

That IS kind of cool.

Kinky but cool.

You are not allowed to sexualize my science.

I promise to do my best not to sexualize your sudden obsessions.

Good. I don't have anyone to talk about this kind of stuff with.

I mean, I guess I could talk to my mom, but that'd be so wrong.

Plus, she'd probably already know it.

And then she'd go into lecture mode.

And then your father would try to share the cool stuff he knows?

Yeah? How'd you know?

I listen to you, remember?

Oh, yeah.

Okay.

Did that freak you out?

A little.

???

I'm not used to people actually listening to me.

Or remembering all the stuff I say.

???

I don't know. Most of my friends get bored long before that point.

And miss all this great stuff?

I'll bet they're even watching David Lynch movies entirely unprotected!

Ha! Lexi probably is.

She and Dylan probably finished Mulholland Drive with a huge case of existential dread.

You IMDb'd that, didn't you?

Yeah.

Really all I know is Dune and Eraserhead

And I don't think ANYTHING can protect you from Eraserhead.

You doubt the powers of acetaminophen?

You have CLEARLY never seen Eraserhead.

You have?

My father thinks watching ancient movies is a form of togetherness.

Do you rip them apart afterward and analyze every little piece as a family?

No.

Oh, just my family, then.

That sounds like actual togetherness.

Well, it can be. Depends on the movie.

And how much we hated it.

Might actually be fun to watch a movie with your family.

**9:14 p.m.**

Still there?

Sorry.

Yeah. But only for a second.

Did freak you out again?

My mom was talking to me, but she went upstairs for something.

Cool.

Really quick . . . what's your schedule like?

Really random, Mr. Office Job.

Afternoons, MWF.

At least for this month.

Then it changes again.

Annoying.

Yeah, I can pick up more shifts, but they have to keep me under a certain amount of hours.

Or benefits kick in???

Exactly.

How'd you know that?

Accountant mother.

Remember?

Well, it's nice you don't just listen to me.

Eep. Gotta go!

Good night, stranger.

Night, weirdo.

## WEDNESDAY, JUNE 8
### 8:37 a.m.

What are you doing?

### 9:28 a.m.

Shouldn't you be working?

Don't worry I'm not driving.

I'm sleeping.

Doesn't sound like sleeping.

Well, this doesn't look like working.

BORED

It's 9:30. You've been working for, what? Half an hour?

I started at 8.

Woo. An hour and a half.

You're why people think our generation can't pay attention for more than five minutes.

I've been sitting in a hallway for an hour waiting for you to wake up.

I lack any more things to pay attention to.

Do you at least have a chair?

I have a nice comfy floor.

Why are you sitting on the floor?

The construction company's owner isn't done with his meeting.

And he can't afford chairs?

CHUCK can

Or my mother wouldn't be dating him.

Mere interns at job sites are not worthy of chairs.

He can splurge on a lawn mower but not chairs?

Don't get me started

His priorities are all kinds of wrong.

Last time I was here I had to stare at his model airplane collection for a solid forty-five minutes.

Were you really still asleep?

Mostly. Technically I'm eating breakfast.

At 9:30???

Your family lets you sleep that long???

Yes. I sleep in at least that long.

You should too.

What'd you read?

It's common knowledge pediatricians recommend teenagers sleep later in the morning and stay up later at night.

It's key for our development and improves mood stability and decision-making.

A LOT of articles is what you're saying.

So many.

You have no idea.

Could you send them to my mother???

I'll leave that to you.

You need to do your own research.

Does she not let you sleep?

She thinks anything past 5 a.m. is "sleeping in."

She doesn't understand the biochemical difference between adolescents and adults.

Focus on the American Association of Pediatrics stuff.

But there might be more going on there.

Has she had HER hormones tested?

Why would her SEVENTEEN-YEAR-OLD SON know that??????

Menstrual health is a highly under-researched area. Menopause affects everyone with a uterus and yet very little is known about it.

Remind me never to wake you up.

It's important, though.

If she has other symptoms like hot flashes, she should really be tested.

Now we're talking about my mother's HOT FLASHES???

I miss being bored!!!!!!!!

Just because your penis is well researched doesn't mean you can't care about your mother's health.

Especially if she's young she could be overlooking many of her period symptoms.

LOOK

THE DOOR IS OPENING

I HAVE TO WORK NOW.

Typical.

**8:45 p.m.**

Quick, tell me someone I should have a celebrity crush on.

???

It's Hump Day. Lexi is threatening to drag me out this weekend if I don't participate in one of her awful quizzes.

And for this you need a celebrity crush?

Who even calls it Hump Day?

Lexi. Well, her dad. He thinks he's clever and she agrees for some reason.

Why am I not surprised Lexi laughs at dad jokes

It's who she is.

But hurry.

Aren't you supposed to have your OWN celebrity crush?

Apparently.

But you don't.

What about your geologist podcast nerds?

A) We discussed this.

B) I don't have a crush on them.

C) She would totally not accept that.

Helping! NOT sexualizing!

What about Ryan Reynolds?

Really?

He's equally funny and cute!

Isn't he a little old?

OK . . . not Ryan Reynolds.

Guess that rules out James McAvoy.

And Fassbender.

What are you doing? Looking at the casts of X-Men movies?

Huh . . . you're right . . .

You're not?

Am now!

Hrm, Ian McKellen has potential.

But RYAN REYNOLDS is too old?????

Oh, right.

But he's just so cute. Especially with Patrick Stewart.

And you think *I* have a type.

What?

Evan Peters???

Nicholas Hoult???

Oh, yeah, War Boy! I'll go with Nux.

Oh right, he WAS in that.

Thanks, you're the best!

You forgot I was a boy again, didn't you?

What?

No, I just needed help.

With a celebrity crush???

And you thought you'd just take one of mine?

Yeah.

There . . . posted.

Glad I could help.

I guess.

I was desperate.

Clearly.

I'm not good at this stuff, okay.

I mean, you didn't do it either.

How would you know if I did this or not???

Oh, right, strangers.

Sorry.

Not that.

Never mind. I'm being stupid.

What? You're not stupid.

You did better than a B on your speech.

We got As and you only got a B???

What was Mrs. James thinking?

Perhaps that I should have strung more than five words together at a time?

You weren't that bad.

Also, something about it being about stating an argument rather than a recitation of facts.

You were robbed.

I could have done better.

My visual aid was lackluster.

I got over interested in the details.

Clearly.

. . .

Are you mad at me?

You sound mad at me.

I'm sorry I didn't get a better grade.

It's not that at all.

Don't worry about it.

Are you sure?

Weren't you in a hurry?

Well, yeah, I gotta go eat.

But I think you're upset.

Eat.

We can talk later.

This isn't important.

You're sure?

I have to come up with a new celebrity crush.

Mine's too old.

Well, good luck with that!

Whatever.

## FRIDAY, JUNE 10
### 8:01 p.m.

You going to Lexi's Friday Funday???

Not now.

You OK?

No.

Family stuff?

No.

OK.

You still awake?

Yeah

Isn't this after plug-in?

Yeah. Well.

I kinda snuck downstairs.

To talk to me?

Couldn't sleep.

You OK?

Yes.

No.

I don't know.

Why are you still awake?

Doing some PvP.

Oh, yeah? Beating everyone else at capture the flag?

Of course you know what PvP is.

No, Jack and I are in a 2v2 with our Horde alts.

Of course.

I probably couldn't take you on even if I DID have a partner, but I'd beat both of you up and down any battleground you choose.

Like you did at the spelling bee?

We both lost that.

I didn't choke on an EASY word.

Look. Judgemental is a super-hard word to remember.

Did it again.

ARGH! Judgmental. Judgmental. Judgmental. Judgmental.

This is not very stranger-ly of you.

Sorry.

No, it's okay. It's kind of nice actually.

???

You know me and still want to talk to me.

Why wouldn't I?

You'd be surprised.

Did you fight with someone?

Sorta.

Anyone I should pretend not to know?

No.

Okay, yes.

I won't ask

It's ridiculous.

I got into a fight with Sarah . . . and Chloe.

???

I guess Chloe recognized the clown's car in the parking lot, so Sarah was giving me the third degree.

You don't have to tell me if you don't want to.

No, I mean, it's embarrassing.

He's been coming in all week.

It's nice your manager just lets maniac clowns roam free like that.

Okay, maybe "maniac" is a bit strong.

Now we're getting somewhere.

Well, right.

That's the problem.

Sarah actually asked if I was dating him.

Can you believe that???

How'd they get that from one drive-by?

Probably from me not insulting him the second his name was mentioned.

The second?

Is that how you usually react?

That's a lot of hate.

I screwed up.

You're too good a friend.

Tell Chloe that.

Trust me I would

But it probably wouldn't help.

Uh, no. Really wouldn't.

In fact, especially act like we're strangers when Sarah and Chloe are around.

Doing my best not to say anything to Chloe these days.

Good, because I don't think she likes me.

She definitely doesn't like me as much as she likes Sarah.

I guess they've been hanging out . . . a lot.

Because that makes sense.

So, yeah. That's why I was upset.

Sorry.

What are you sorry for? It's not your fault.

It's a little my fault.

How? You're a stranger that lives halfway across nowhere.

Right sorry

This Chloe sounds a bit . . .

Yeah I don't know what word to use without you getting mad.

She's a bit spoiled.

But she's super smart.

And Sarah seems to really like her.

And if the price of keeping both of them happy is not liking someone who has nothing to do with me, so what?

So you don't ACTUALLY hate him?

I don't know.

I mean, before you and I started talking? A little.

Now?

I am willing to sell him burritos.

All to keep Chloe happy?

Why??? So she won't be mean to you?

I don't know.

It's easier.

For you or her?

For Sarah?

Doesn't sound like you want to.

I want to. I mean, he did break my best friend's heart into a thousand pieces once.

If he hadn't betrayed Chloe the same way he did Sarah, things wouldn't be this bad.

???

You know about the other girl?

At camp?

The one he cheated on Sarah with.

HE cheated on HER?

Yeah? Didn't you know?

I can honestly say I've never heard this before.

He started liking someone else, and when Sarah confronted him about it, he just stopped talking to her entirely.

No closure, nothing. Just cold shoulder.

That's what she told you?

I mean, I get why they're both upset.

It hurts when someone doesn't like you back.

But does that mean you have to keep punishing someone when they don't have anything to do with it?

How is this punishment? It's not like he even knows I exist beyond nasty burritos.

Have YOU liked someone who didn't like you back?

EVERYONE I've liked hasn't liked me back.

I've never managed to like anyone who COULD like me back.

If I can like the wrong person at the wrong time, that's the only person I'll like.

And I can never tell anyone because it's way too late and everything about it is wrong.

I can screw up any chance at a relationship. It kinda comes with being me.

What do you mean?

I'm a freak.

You've seen it.

I can make anything awkward. I like everything too much. I know more than any human should about things no one cares about.

I barely speak aloud.

Even my friends don't want to spend time with me.

The only reason YOU talk to me is because we're texting.

You would NEVER talk to me if it wasn't texting.

No, you never DID talk to me before texting.

You still haven't.

You are not a freak.

HA!

I mean it

You're interesting

You know the coolest stuff.

Tho I'd rather not know about menopause.

See! I make anything awkward.

A little

But you're not terrible.

You don't manipulate people.

Who else am I going to talk to the next time I have to babysit clay?

Weirdo.

I'm messed up too you know.

Oh, right. The handsome, rich, famous, charming, clever guy who also happens to be smart is messed up too.

That's not me.

Everyone disagrees.

You were so perfect the universe basically cloned you.

Ugh, no one wants to be anything like me.

You really think that way?

And cocky. Ugh, this is not about you right now!!!!

I suck at this.

What do you want me to do?

I just want you to agree with me.

Can't . . . sorry.

Why not?

Nothing you've said is true.

MAYBE that I'm perfect . . .

But sorry I didn't talk to you before.

No, you're not.

You were quiet so I thought you were shy.

Like catatonic.

But I could tell you were paying attention to everything

Like all the time.

It's intimidating.

Great. Even you're afraid of me.

Not afraid of you.

Well

I was

Of course.

BUT!!!

Now I kind of like it.

Because I distract you when you're bored.

Not anymore!

Learned that lesson the hard way.

You didn't even want to talk to me after that.

That's not it!

It's been two days.

Last night was forced family time with my mother and CHUCK who can have me fired.

He took us to this ridiculously expensive sushi place

We had an entire table full of fish.

You don't have to make excuses.

I'm not!

It's fine. You don't have to talk to me.

Haley

Listen to me.

I'm telling the truth.

I should probably go to bed. My dad might wake up and check on me.

Fine don't listen.

I need to go.

Just, one thing.

What's that?

Don't message me after we say good night.

Why not?

Because I don't want to miss it.

AND because my mom will hear and wake up.

She'll hear your phone?

On vibrate.

From a dead sleep.

That's like superhuman.

Normal moms wake up when their teenagers sneak downstairs, she wakes up at cell phones.

On VIBRATE?

Superpower.

Tell me about it.

Okay, so, night.

Good night, Haley

And Haley's super mother.

**10:42 a.m.**

Sorry about last night.

You didn't need that.

At brunch

WILL TALK LATER.

**3:12 p.m.**

Sorry . . . we had bonus Saturday family time today.

No, it's fine. I said what I wanted to say.

I haven't.

I was just tired. It wasn't anything big.

I'm sorry you had to deal with it.

Want to tell me what really happened?

It was stupid.

Sarah overheard heard someone say your cousin has someone new. She and Chloe decided they needed to warn his latest victim first.

Then Chloe mentioned seeing his car at the gas station.

I don't know what she thinks she saw. He was just buying a freaking burrito.

So they overreacted.

I did. You didn't need that.

Just pretend it didn't happen.

Would you stop saying that?

Sorry.

Stop apologizing.

You OK now?

Yeah. I'm fine.

But are you mad at me?

No. Why?

I just . . .

ARGH!

I'm glad you talked to me last night.

Really?

You not talking to me would worry me.

I'm sorry.

No, I mean, I won't bother you with that stuff anymore.

That's the opposite of what I meant.

No, it's fine.

I'm glad you told me what happened

I wanted to know why you were upset.

You don't have to say that just because I had a bad day.

Like I say things just to make you happy.

Good point!

You can talk to me when you feel like that.

I don't need you to make everything better. This isn't really about Chloe.

It's not even about Sarah.

It's my brain. You can't fix that.

I can try.

No, don't try.

I don't want that kind of help.

???

Last night was about being in my head all the time. Every second of the day. Always. Forever.

I just couldn't sleep.

Just don't stop talking to me

No matter what happens.

Promise?

You say that now.

You think you have a corner on bad days?

Overly dramatic bad days? Yes. All mine. No one else can have any.

Wait until my next bad day and I guarantee you'll be impressed.

You're scheduling bad days in advance?

We're traveling next week

There are plenty of bad days ahead.

Oh, that sucks.

I thought vacations were all about fun.

You have never been on vacation with my father

And his wife

Pre-divorce.

Where are you going?

Paris.

How tragic.

The nicer the place the worse it gets.

I'm taking odds on whether or not he compares her to a Rubens or Madame Defarge.

Why not both?

I like the way you think.

Sorry, that was mean.

We have to laugh or we cry

And we're too manly to cry.

Well, I may be. I don't know about you.

Touché.

## MONDAY, JUNE 13
### 11:28 a.m.

So, are you already gone?

### 3:54 p.m.

Not until Friday.

### 7:57 p.m.

Oh, I was just wondering.

You'll be glad to know your text came in as I was driving and I didn't even look near it.

Good. Texting and driving is ridiculously bad for your health.

Today has SUUUUUUUUUCKED.

More mysterious phyllosilicates?

Everyone forgot things EVERYWHERE I went.

I went back and forth to each job site like five times.

Oh, poor you.

You get a day off tomorrow

I get to complain a bit.

You are going to Paris, you get to complain not at all.

You like Paris?

I thought you did German.

And Spanish and a TINY bit of Korean.

I always wanted to learn French.

You know three languages?

Four, you forgot English. But I'm only actually any good at English.

How'd you manage that many?

Spanish in junior high and German in high school.

Why didn't you stick with Spanish?

Didn't feel like it.

I wanted to learn German.

Where'd you learn Korean?

TV and family.

My aunt IS Korean and my uncle is fluent.

Is your family why you watch their TV?

It's how I know their TV exists. But I watch it because it's awesome.

So I pick up a little from my family and a little from TV and I'm almost okay at some of it.

I know how to order food and listen to someone complain about their mother-in-law.

Does your aunt complain about her mother-in-law?

HAH! No! That part's from TV.

Got it.

But you're not getting off the topic this easily.

???

You're going to freaking France.

?????

I WANNA GO!

THAT'S what this is about . . .

You could fit me in your luggage, right?

Considering how much luggage Step2 is bringing that shouldn't be a problem.

YES!

Croissants and baguettes here I come.

Bread?

You want to hide in the belly of a plane for bread?

YES! And desserts and the Musée d'Orsay and the Louvre and Versailles.

We're not going to Versailles this time.

I would be a stowaway. I could go anywhere I want.

Not the Eiffel Tower?

I mean, I'd look at it, but not really.

You got something against Monsieur Eiffel?

No, he was doing his thing.

I'm just not a big fan of tourist traps.

You're calling the GREATEST feat of 1800s engineering a TOURIST TRAP???

Well, yeah.

I mean, it serves no purpose. It was built for the world's fair.

That's basically the definition of a tourist trap.

You do NOT get to come to Paris!

OMG, it's just iron.

It's a symbol of freedom.

It's a wannabe bridge that goes nowhere.

IT'S SPARKLY!

You were never taking me to Paris anyway.

I was never taking you to Paris.

But you'll get me something, though, right?

What would I get you?

I don't know. Something so Paris it hurts.

That's woefully specific and vague all at the same time.

I'd rather have nothing than something generic.

No Eiffel Tower snow globes?

UGH! No!

No shot glasses either!

No shot glasses.

I can't imagine you drinking anyway.

Yeah, me neither. I mean, I'm sure I will one day.

When it's legal and aboveboard.

When it's a safe space and I feel ready.

So responsible it hurts.

I should tattoo that on my forehead.

You should!!!

Okay, you're leaving Friday. How long are you going to be gone?

Ten days.

So, the next Sunday?

Monday.

Oh, so ten days in Paris.

Yeah

Isn't it strange your parents are taking you to a really romantic European city?

If it were a genuine vacation . . . maybe.

It's not really a vacation?

It's an investor meeting.

We get to dog and pony the heck out of it.

So suits, ties, and combed hair?

There's even a gala.

Poor thing.

You don't get it.

Clearly.

I'm basically an accessory.

I have to talk to everyone

All the time

Smile constantly

Pretend I care about which harbor they keep their yacht

The Mediterranean yacht of course

The American yacht they keep at the house . . . Obviously.

Obviously. They're not animals.

Okay, yes, I can see how that might not be the most amazing way to see Europe.

It's more than that.

. . .

I can't explain in a way you'll understand.

Actually, I think I kind of get it.

???

Lexi.

I love her, but every once in a while I get the feeling I'm more like a project than a friend.

What do you mean?

Well, she always needs to have something going on and every so often *I* am that thing.

Like she has to fix me.

That's sort of it.

No, I mean FIX me. Like when things get bad.

She dresses me up. Takes me to parties.

Makes me socialize.

Fix you up with Jack?

URGH! Strangers would not know about him.

But sorta.

You might KINDA get it.

Not perfect, but yeah.

So . . .

Okay, what one thing are you going to do while you're there?

I just told you all the things I have to do.

No. It's something my mom does. She has us all pick a thing we want to do.

Nothing expensive or fancy or really complicated.

Just one really easy thing to do that will guarantee the trip will be a success.

???

Like when we went to LA, she wanted to see the Hollywood sign because one time she made it a whole trip without seeing it.

Seeing the sign?

From anywhere???

Yeah, from anywhere.

That's a low bar.

We're low-bar kind of people.

But, even if it's raining or everyone's sick, you pick one little thing and be sure to do at least that.

That's actually kind of cool

And with our well-scheduled agenda . . . necessary.

So, what's it going to be? Coffee on the Left Bank? Spitting into the Seine? Something Awful Tower related?

I want a selfie at Notre Dame.

Oooh. Very religious.

Very Quasimodo.

Did you have a crush on Esmeralda?

I REALLY liked that movie when I was little! My grandparents had a copy and I watched it about a thousand times.

The cartoon one?

Of course!

Isn't that generally agreed to be the worst movie ever?

Hush your mouth!!! Quasimodo will hear you!!!

I'm sorry.

I'm not making fun of you. I'm just . . .

Surprised?

I'm going to Notre Dame and your mockery will not stop me.

I'm not trying to mock you.

But do you think you'll make it? Considering your schedule?

It shouldn't be too hard

Our hotel is mere BLOCKS from there.

Don't tell me. I don't think I want to know.

You probably don't.

You're probably an Oscar Wilde fangirl.

You mean the hotel where he died???????

It's not too late for me to hate you again.

Don't forget none of this is my choice.

Well, if you want me not to hate you, I thought of one thing you could do for me . . .

I'm not kissing his tomb.

No, there's a bookstore near Notre Dame.

Won't the books be in French?

No, smarty-pants, there's a famous English language bookstore near there called Shakespeare and Company.

It's LITERALLY on the way to Notre Dame from your hotel.

You want an ENGLISH book from FRANCE?

No.

Would you smell it for me?

You want me to SMELL a bookstore?

Yes. I want to know if it smells like the old book room in the downtown library.

You want me to tell you if a store

With hundreds of old books

Smells like old books???

I just need to know that I'm imagining it right.

You are an odd duck

But if it means you won't hate me . . .

AND it's LITERALLY across the river from Notre Dame, Quasimodo.

THE BELLS! THE BELLS!

You are no longer allowed to call me an odd anything.

I will smell your bookstore but you have to do something for me too.

Uh. What?

I want a story when I get back.

A story?

You need to have a wacky adventure while I'm gone

And you HAVE to tell me about it.

You want me to have a wacky adventure?

Wacky enough to be entertaining.

Uh, okay. I think I can manage that.

You can definitely manage it.

You have to tell me what happens. Like if your dad takes a French lover. Or your stepmom. Or both could get taken in by the same con woman!!!

Thank you for THOSE visuals.

Sorry, you're the one who got me on wacky.

That's not wacky . . . that's wrong!

Just think, if you're really lucky, Step3 could be European.

Not funny.

OMG, it's already time.

We've been talking forever.

Okay, I'll probably talk to you again before you go.

You will

Don't worry.

I'm not worrying!

Yeah right.

Don't need help with Hump Day?

Nah, this week I've got it.

What was the question this time?

Relationship goals.

Couples you've got

But individuals not so much?

Who'd you pick?

Stucky?

No. Nothing so pedestrian.

I picked the Obamas.

Good choice.

Who'd you pick?

Haven't done it.

Well, who WOULD you pick?

Other than your parents?

Ew.

I mean it.

So gross. No give me a real answer.

I don't know. You took the best one.

Except for Chloe, who picked
F. Scott Fitzgerald and Zelda.

WHY? Was Bonnie and Clyde already taken?

It was! By Sarah!

Zelda sounds about right for Chloe, but I expected more from Sarah.

Chloe WOULD make a good Jazz Age maven.

I take it you haven't pointed out the later part of the Fitzgeralds' relationship?

You mean the institutionalizations?

No, I'm done making those two mad.

...

Don't you dare.

I haven't done ANYTHING!

No teasing my friends.

I'd never tease a friend of yours.

Shouldn't you be packing or something?

Or something.

I don't want to keep you.

You're not keeping me.

I mean, I have to go take a shower and get this gas station grunge off me.

Do that.

Okay, I will.

I HATE PACKING!!!

### 5:08 p.m.

You leave tomorrow!!! Why are you still packing?

I'm not STILL packing

I AM packing.

I'm going to pack.

Packing will have happened.

What if you forget something?

That's why the concierge desk was invented.

I'm sure YOU have a whole method for packing.

AS A MATTER OF FACT I DO.

???

PACK EARLIER!

That's not it and you and I both know it.

You probably have it down to the specific items you'll pack.

What? Oh look, is that the television calling?

YOU DO!!!

Well, you need at least eleven pairs of underwear and eleven pairs of socks.

And that's all I'm saying about your unmentionables.

We haven't even begun to mention my unmentionables.

No one is mentioning their unmentionables further or I'm not helping!

Consider them unmentioned.

Okay, so, you have events?

Every day

All day

Into the night

First thing in the morning

All the time

Until my smile is permanently etched on my face.

Or the zombie apocalypse

Whichever comes first.

What are we talking about? You said gala.

One formal event

Two cocktail parties

And one boat cruise.

A freaking cruise along the Seine?

No focusing on how lucky I am to cruise down a smelly river with a hundred old drunks.

Oh, right, poor, poor baby.

You CLEARLY have never had your unmentionables discussed at length by women as old as your grandmother.

This is true, but right now I'm more worried about the fact you're going to need boat shoes.

You don't actually care about me at all

Do you?

I care about no one going to a European capital tomorrow and not knowing where his first aid kit is.

You travel with a first aid kit?

Of course! You don't?

I'll put some Band-Aids in my bag.

OMG, you're useless.

Okay, so back to formal clothes. Do you have a suit?

Step2 bought me two new ones.

They're in a garment bag in the corner.

Hanging in the corner?

Oh, wait, no, don't answer that.

I wouldn't tell you even if you threatened me.

I'm now more afraid of you than I am of my grandmother.

Well, that's at least something.

Okay, shoes. Did she buy you shoes too?

They're these shiny black things with the smallest laces you've ever seen.

In general you'll also need slip-on shoes and comfortable walking shoes.

But the boat shoes should work for slip-ons. Wear those, pack the other two.

Shouldn't I wear the comfortable shoes???

How many times have you been on long-haul flights?

Ten-ish.

Well, I've only been on four, but clearly I'm better at it than you.

Wear the slip-ons so you can take them off.

On the plane?

Yes! It's way more comfortable.

But more importantly for getting through security.

You're a freaking genius.

Of course I am.

So, pants.

Two pairs of shorts, one pair of pants.

Or vice versa.

Or three pairs of pants, or whatever.

For ten days?

Yeah, they're pants. Worst-case scenario you have your fancy concierge launder them for you for a billion euros.

The exchange rate isn't THAT bad.

But carry on.

I'm more interested in the "Haley Hancock Method of Overseas Packing" (TM)

I don't need to register intellectual property if it's electronically documented like this.

But shirts!!!

I intend on wearing them yes.

Well, good. I like to pack way more T-shirts than days I'll be gone.

Seems excessive compared to your pants philosophy.

My mom is a shirt minimalist, but I do not agree with her premise.

I like having a clean shirt to sleep in, so I throw in a few extra.

That's pretty much it. Isn't it?

Shoes

Unmentionables

Pants

Shirts

For a guy, yes.

But don't forget to pack stuff for the plane.

Like my iPad and charger?

Yes, but also get a magazine.

A magazine?

You mean the paper kind?

You know what those are???

Yes, I know what paper magazines are.

And they're awesome for plane rides.

I'm still talking to Haley . . . right?

Haley Hancock?

Soon to be high school senior?

Having something that doesn't glow, or beep, or vibrate can be nice.

You're big on sensory aren't you?

Not usually, but at the seven-hour point, when I can't sleep and can't stare at another screen, I like it.

I'll get a magazine tomorrow.

Also put everything in your carry-on when you leave the house.

NOTHING in your pockets.

You're also one of those people who sneers at anyone who slows down the TSA line.

SO MUCH!

WHY CAN THEY NEVER BE PREPARED?

You must be a JOY to travel with.

I'm a fricking delight!

A little forethought makes the whole process easier.

You're like the Mary Poppins of air travel.

For your peace of mind I will attempt forethought.

Also, put some spare euros in random spots in your bags.

Pickpockets? Really? You think black cars and five-star hotels have pickpockets?

I think it's better safe than sorry.

Actually it would be a really good idea

If only I had euros

You don't have a safe with foreign currency pre-converted at advantageous rates?

Who does that???

Your grampa.

I read an article about it once.

Of course you did!

My father can't plan ahead like that.

Well, then, you should consider taking after his father instead.

But do it when we're older.

Keeping a safe with euros seems excessive for an unpaid intern.

A bit

Thank you for acknowledging seventeen-year-olds don't require liquid assets.

I do try to be mindful.

People would think I'M the one who has no grasp on reality

Oh, whatever.

Go pack.

Oui, mademoiselle.

And have fun or I'll choke you with a dusty gas station croissant.

Not even a burrito?

TOO GOOD FOR YOU!

Don't forget your promise.

Yes, yes, wacky antics. I'm on it.

And, Haley

What?

Nothing.

Goodbye, Martin.

Au revoir, Haley.

## FRIDAY, JUNE 24
### 11:45 p.m.

I know you're still in Paris.

I hope you're having fun.

I just . . .

I wish you were here.

## MONDAY, JUNE 27
### 8:47 a.m.

Bonjour, mon amie!

I AM ON AMERICAN SOIL!!!

Not ON soil

On American tarmac

Which is basically the same thing.

Not quite ON the tarmac

In a plane on the tarmac.

I haven't slept in 24 hours

But got my second wind so that's something.

You're probably still asleep.

I'm still halfway across the country

Just wanted to tell you I'm back.

### 10:59 a.m.

We're through customs

Through security

About to get on our domestic flight.

I expected you'd be awake by now.

I have so much to tell you.

If you say something after this I won't answer because I'll be on yet another plane.

But home soon.

**3:48 p.m.**

I AM IN YOUR TIME ZONE!

Muahaha third wind.

I totally have this.

Not losing my mind.

You're at work. Right?

We're once more taxiing.

I'm not worried.

It's totally fine that you haven't answered me yet.

You're busy.

But you're not going to believe what happened.

**5:48 p.m.**

Home!!!

Home-home.

Yet I still haven't heard from you

So now I'm kind of worried.

Especially after Friday.

Please answer?

What happened???

**7:05 p.m.**

This is Haley's mother. She explained you're someone she met online who has been overseas for a while.

Haley is perfectly fine.

She's taking some time to consider the consequences of her actions.

While this means she may not use her phone, she asked me to say that her story will be requisitely wacky for you and that you should not be concerned.

She will be permitted to speak to you again on Thursday, barring any unforeseen extensions of her punishment.

We all hope you had a pleasant trip.

# THURSDAY, JUNE 30
## 1:03 p.m.

I'M FREE!

FINALLY FREE! OMG, FREE!

But I'm at a con.

So answer when you can, but I may be spotty.

## 4:59 p.m.

You got your phone back and immediately went out to break the law?

What happened while I was in France???

Not that kind of con.

A fan convention at the big hotel near the airport.

The kind with panels and cosplay and time spent with my fellow nerds.

Your mother took away your phone instead of grounding you from a convention?

It's a family tradition.

But SHE didn't.

She DIDN'T let you go??? You snuck into that too?

No, she didn't take away my phone. My dad did. Mom thinks going without technology goes against the Geneva Conventions.

Yet she let him take away your phone in the first place?

She also believes in not undermining her spouse. So while she disagreed philosophically, she did nothing to stop it.

So you pissed off your father?

More freaked him out.

He doesn't get angry, he gets scared and then freaks and then does things and then regrets them. And in between are the lectures.

Soliloquies really on his reasoning behind what he did and what I should learn from each given situation.

My mom gets mad, but she's more psychological about it.

Eternal guilt rather than hard labor or restrictions.

Sounds painful.

Could be worse.

Trust me.

I do.

You see

YOU still have the full complement of parents you started the month with

While I'm down one parental unit.

Oh! Did something happen?

Nothing news van worthy.

Step2 opted to remain in France to "develop relationships" with "overseas investors."

Okay, I get the scare quotes on the first part.

What am I supposed to infer from the second?

That I may not actually know how to use scare quotes.

Let's just say my father decided to interview "au pairs" while we were abroad

Fancy nannies? I didn't know you had siblings.

I don't . . .

Oh.

OOOOOH!

Oh no! I'm so sorry!

Not like it was a surprise.

You called it before we left.

I never in a million years thought it'd be real.

This is what he does.

It was already bad

He just exploded it.

Yeah, I get that.

It is what it is.

Are you okay? Like, is he okay?

I'm at my mother's now.

Except she ALSO broke up with her boyfriend.

The one who wants you to like him?

Oh man. She must be so sad.

Worse.

What's worse than sad?

My father has also opted to spend the weekend at my mother's.

And that's bad?

Worse than a nineteen-year-old au pair for your seventeen-year-old son.

She was nineteen?!?

And Swiss.

That's so skeezy!

I told you

Explosions

Now he has to pull everyone into the blast radius.

So we're in the revenge-hookup/booty-call/vomit-inducing parent together time that may now officially be considered a tradition.

At least until THAT explodes

All over me.

Oh, that's awful.

I have a large closet if you'd like to run away from home.

I may take you up on that.

I'll move some of my clothes.

What about you?

What about me?

Why were you separated from your phone for four days?

Six days.

Six days?

Is this related to one of Lexi's Friday Fundays???

It's ridiculous. You won't want to hear it.

Your mother said it was requisitely wacky.

She did not. Did she really say "requisitely"?

She did.

Oh no! She did!!! So embarrassing!

But you're trying to distract me from what I really want to know.

Caught that, did you?

Not going to work.

Okay, fine. Before you get the story though, I need to know you're ready to compensate me for it.

Musty

Tired

Warm

A little like the river

But also like almonds.

Mmmmmmmm.

Three different tourists took a picture of me smelling the place.

It was so embarrassing.

What did you do, walk in the door and just breathe?

Yes!

Weirdo. You could have gone into a corner.

You wanted the authentic experience!

I want the authentic experience for myself!

I'm stuck living vicariously through you.

Though, imagining you smelling a bookstore is kinda hilarious.

Trust me

However you're imagining it is wrong.

You didn't, by chance, get one of those other tourists' pictures of you . . . did you?

No . . . I sent you a postcard instead.

I know! I got it! Freaked my mom out.

A postcard freaked your mother out?

She thought it was junk mail.

She was trying to figure out why a French bookstore was trying to market to me.

Your mother read my postcard.

Well, yeah, that's the thing about non-tech. Everyone can see it.

I didn't say anything embarrassing

Right?

Nope, just something about the Awful Tower.

We went to the top.

Paris was both very large and very small from there.

I thought you weren't going to have time for touristing.

It wasn't touristing.

Turns out they have a champagne bar up there.

Schmoozing at the top?

Monsieur Eiffel did not plan for ladies in fancy dresses at the top in the wind

But they were all happy pointing out various tryst locations in the city for me as they held down their skirts.

Ewww. Well, I had to hear all about how Mom knew someone who knew someone or was related to someone who lived near there.

Sounds . . .

Don't try to describe my family. Slippery slope.

If you don't try to describe mine.

Never!

Tell me your wacky adventure.

Later. Panel's starting.

I am so freaking tired.

I just have to point out

You texted me this early

I did not text you

I do not need to be told anything about anyone's hormones.

I'm too tired for that. Plus, my brain is full of nerd.

Worse than usual?

WAY WORSE!

You have no idea.

Why are you awake already?

Nerding! I told you.

That con?

Yeah.

Are you in cosplay?

Uh, no. I mean, I've got my wig and some makeup on, but I'm not a cosplayer.

My parents' friends are. They're way cool.

A bunch of them are coming as Drunken Sailors today.

Navy?

Sailor Moon.

You mean anime?

Yeah, the Sailor Jupiter is on point.

I think I need to see that.

You wish you were that lucky.

I have to work now

But you ARE going to tell me about your wacky antics today.

Oh, yeah, after this panel.

You said that last time.

Sorry, I got distracted.

I really mean it this time.

How long will this panel take?

An hour.

Same as my run.

Okay, later.

**9:30 a.m.**

Sorry, that went long. I promise I'm not avoiding you. I went to get some tea.

Tea?

Yeah, I like tea? You gonna make something of it?

Sorry too busy

I'm getting in my car.

Again?

Some of us work for a living.

They're not even paying you.

Some people waste their lives for invaluable business experience they can put on their résumé.

Okay, drive safe.

Always!

**12:04 p.m.**

Lunchtime!

**12:19 p.m.**

I'll skip my next panel for you.

Anything good?

Not that I want you to go

You've already put me off forever.

Ehn, it was only okay.

They were talking about dystopians and I've already read all those.

You don't want to talk about them?

You usually like talking about the things you read.

If they went for Thomas More, I could get behind it.

You are NOT distracting me with English philosophers!!!!!!!!

Spill.

Okay, fine.

So, Sarah, Chloe, and Lexi came over.

Was it a wild party?

Do you want the story or not?

Just help me out here

Did you have a pillow fight?

YOU ARE NOT GETTING A STORY.

I'll be good.

Proper expectations have now been set.

Go on.

I'll be good!!!

Promise!!!!!

Okay, so, Sarah, Chloe, and Lexi came over to watch some Netflix.

What'd you watch?

Nothing important.

What IS important is that we wanted pancakes.

Who doesn't want pancakes?

I know, right?

Okay, so my mom had said it was all right if I drove her car.

What kind of car?

A Camry.

An old lady car?

Yeah, but I like it. More importantly, it's an automatic.

. . .

Right.

So, she and my dad went somewhere. I don't even know where. But they were gone . . .

In her car.

Why?

They always take Mom's car.

Your mother lets your father drive her car?

Uh, no. She drives.

Your father lets your mother drive him around?

"Lets" is a very strong word.

"Accepts that if he wants to go anywhere with her, she'll be driving" is a better way to put it.

If you were anyone else . . . I'd be confused

But I think this is starting to make sense.

I told you, we're special.

Go on.

So, I had permission. Just not for Dad's car. But we REALLY needed chocolate chip pancakes. It was vital.

Pancakes often are.

CHOCOLATE CHIP pancakes.

Sorry

Chocolate chip pancakes always are.

What's the deal with your father's car?

It's .,. .

Uh . . .

It's a stick.

You do or do not know how to drive a manual transmission?

I have practiced driving a manual in a very empty parking lot.

Did you hit something?

In the parking lot? No.

I don't mean in the parking lot.

I may have, kinda, sorta, a little bit, nudged the garage door slightly.

You didn't!!!

Lexi was yelling at me to push the "handle" while Sarah and Chloe would NOT shut up in the back seat.

I got so confused I pressed down on the gearshift and couldn't even tell I'd finally gotten the car in reverse.

It hadn't been, I swear, my foot only came off the brake for like half a second before I popped it back into neutral!

You OK?

Everyone's okay. Everything's okay.

Except the door. It's kinda bent and it was hard to open.

Dad had to knock it back into shape.

What about the car???

Did you hurt his poor car?

You mean his crappy Jetta? No.

Okay.

A little.

But not enough to notice unless you're really looking hard.

You hurt his car AND the garage?

It's not my fault!

It's Chloe and Sarah's!

They were making so much noise and bouncing around!

And Lexi for not even knowing the difference between a gearshift and a handle.

They distracted me!!!

You couldn't even get the car in gear?

Nothing made sense.

The car wasn't going anywhere, which is good because I knew the sound wasn't right.

I was freaking out because nothing was doing what it was supposed to.

All the while they were chanting "Pancakes" and laughing in the back seat and I knew I couldn't disappoint anyone.

Because chocolate chip pancakes.

Right!

Well, as we were all staring at the very minuscule damage, my parents came home.

Uh-oh.

I didn't have a chance to turn the car off or push it back where it goes or figure out something to do about the door.

And, thus, my dad freaked.

Sounds like everyone freaked.

Mom didn't. Well, she probably did after, but she was really calm.

She tried to calm Dad down too, but he'd already said no phone for a week.

That sucks.

Yeah, but it could have been worse.

Mom drove Chloe, Sarah, and Lexi home.

No pancakes?

No pancakes. But there was no way I was ever going out after that anyway.

Your parents were THAT upset?

No, I was THAT freaked out. Like worse than Dad.

He came into my room later and explained he was more worried about me having an accident without him.

And then he wanted to take me practicing.

Late at night?

No.

Later.

But I'm not ready.

I was so freaked out.

Still kinda am.

Like, crying a little just telling you about it.

I don't want to drive his crappy car again.

That doesn't sound like you.

What? Avoiding horrible things?

Giving up on a challenge.

No one needs to drive a manual.

They're unnecessarily complicated.

You're totally giving up.

I'm not giving up!

Are too.

What? Like you can drive a manual?

In fact I can.

Figures.

You shouldn't give up.

I'll think about it.

That means you'll do it.

Was this story wacky enough for you?

You didn't even make it out of your garage . . .

Yeah. I probably should have tried harder.

You tried hard enough.

I'll count it as wacky

Especially with Sarah and Chloe involved.

Well, good.

Look, I have to go. It's almost time for the next panel.

While I must deliver the updated door measurements to the custom design troll to complete this quest.

Not how this works.

Hush. I'm arming my blunderbuss.

Not how any of this works!

## 7:45 p.m.

I've completed my internship dailies and was granted freedom after earning my ice cream achievement.

Where'd you get ice cream?

From my mother

She took me to the parlor we used to go to when I was little to "have a chat."

Uh-oh. More scare quotes.

That chat wasn't BAD.

We're going to fireworks Monday

With my father.

Ick. Fireworks.

But that doesn't sound scare quote worthy.

. . .

We'll see.

What are you learning about next?

Time travel.

How to?

Why not.

Moral implications?

Nah, no one here cares about that.

More how it's just flat-out ridiculously impossible.

That seems

I don't know

Antithetical to a geek discussion?

Yes and no.

You don't understand my people.

Explain to me your ways.

Well, we like to argue about things that are impossible.

I've experienced this.

So, okay, this is kind of one of my mom's things.

She calls it "controlling for variables."

Like in math?

Yeah, kinda.

Sorta like limits in calculus, only for social situations or for impossible physics stuff.

Ewwww . . . summer calculus.

Well, it's imaginary calculus.

Isn't all calculus imaginary?

Theoretical isn't imaginary.

But some numbers are imaginary.

You're imaginary.

Never mind, you don't deserve my culture.

I really don't.

So what's your deal with fireworks?

I'm against them.

Any reason?

Other than the loud part?

How about the dangerous part?

They're not THAT dangerous.

How about the exploding part?

Sparklers? You can't possibly hate sparklers.

I don't HATE sparklers.

But?

Don't really see the point of them.

The point is that they sparkle!

Yeah.

And?

I'm not sure if I'm ever going to entirely get you.

Nope, still wrapped in bacon.

Mmmmmm . . . bacon.

See?

So, what are you doing this weekend?

Dunno.

Family time

Sitting around

Might check out stuff happening around town

Not going to Chloe's epic party?

Jack said a bunch of everybody is going

Tomorrow night, right?

Sarah definitely is, and Lexi is still deciding, I guess.

What about you?

And miss Masquerade? No way!

Is that a ball???

Do you wear a frilly dress and dance with masked strangers?

No, I sit in the back and watch people who are dressed like anime and Disney characters walk the runway.

This sounds equally fun?

About what I'd be doing at Chloe's, but with more people I like . . . but maybe fewer princesses.

Touché.

Okay, gotta go. Time for another panel.

Talk to you later I guess.

# SATURDAY, JULY 2
## 9:15 a.m.

WHY IS YOUR COUSIN HERE?

My cousin ISN'T there.

Oh, right.

WHY IS THE BURRITO CLOWN HERE?

Is it possible your clown exchanged money for a ticket?

He's been known to do such things in the past.

It's a badge, not a ticket.

He purchased a badge then.

He's sitting in my session. He's like two rows in front of me.

Is there a law against this?

No, but . . .

No.

???

It's just weird.

Why would he come to MY CON?

Maybe he's interested in your culture.

He's not even paying attention. He's playing with his phone.

And what are you doing?

This is different!

Really?

You're useless.

Entirely.

**11:19 a.m.**

He sat next to me the whole last session.

That sounds terrible for you.

Do you think he's stalking me?

I thought maybe you'd said something to him after that Sarah and Chloe thing because I hadn't seen him in a while. But then he was back at the store on Wednesday.

And he was being really strange, like he had something to say, but didn't.

Now he's here.

You have to admit, it's not totally irrational.

Or he figured that since you knew each other it would be less awkward to sit together?

That's what he said.

But do you think he meant it?

Why wouldn't he mean it?

I don't know.

I don't know anything.

It's definitely not less awkward.

Why didn't you tell the burrito clown you hate him and run away?

I couldn't. We talked about the session instead.

And he didn't betray you or any of your friends in ANY way?

No, but I really have no clue what he's doing here.

He'd never even heard of Orphan Black.

I had to tell him who Helena was.

Poor dope.

You don't even know who Helena is, do you?

I do now.

Google doesn't count.

Where is he?

Do you have eyes on?

No, and stop using gamer terms, it's nerdier than I am.

He went to get lunch I think.

Probably eating a burrito.

Probably.

Let me know if he comes back.

I hope not.

He has literally been following me around all afternoon.

You're probably the only person he knows.

I am. It's sad. He gets absolutely nothing.

You're not going to gamer sessions.

Burrito clowns know a lot more about gaming.

Then he should go to those and leave me alone!

Did you ditch him?

No, I'm in the bathroom.

You're texting me from the toilet?

Ew, no, this is a populated place with limited restroom facilities and I'm deeply uncomfortable around urinals.

???

I'm in line, duh.

Ahhhh.

But what about you?

What about me?

How are things going with your parents?

Don't know.

What?

I left the house early this morning rather than watch the fuse burn.

You ditched them?

I guess.

Are YOU going to ditch HIM?

No, he's just so lost.

He's like a puppy.

Poor puppy burrito clown.

Ha, yeah.

It doesn't sound like he's even going to Chloe's party later.

But EVERYONE'S going to Chloe's party.

Har, har.

Fine, it's still just weird.

Like, I don't know what to talk to him about.

What do you talk to me about?

That's not the same.

You'd be surprised.

**7:20 p.m.**

How's your night going?

**7:49 p.m.**

Not what I was expecting.

Same here.

I'm still with the burrito clown.

He keeps asking who people are.

Isn't that what you're supposed to do at these things?

Yeah, but . . .

I'm kinda making stuff up.

You're giving bad info?

I mean, I mostly know who everyone is, at least where they're from.

Sorta.

I don't feel so bad anymore

About what?

Nothing.

He went to the bathroom.

Maybe he'll ditch me.

Doubt it.

How did this become my life?

You only have yourself to blame.

URGH.

## SUNDAY, JULY 3
### 9:28 a.m.

He came back!

Isn't today the last day?

Yeah. I figured he was just pulling a tourist.

Or would at least have to go to church or something.

Maybe he's genuinely interested

Or maybe he got time off for good behavior.

He's texting again.

I'm not even going to dignify that.

### 10:48 a.m.

Kill me now!

My parents found out about him.

This is how I die.

Mortification.

Oh, you're probably at church.

Still.

If I'm dead when you get back, avenge me.

### 12:01 p.m.

Your mother's nice.

THAT'S ALL YOU HAVE TO SAY?

. . .

It's not as bad as you think?

THEY INVITED HIM TO EAT WITH US.

You already know he's capable of that!!!

We're getting pizza.

Not burritos.

He may not survive.

What teenage boy doesn't eat pizza?

You are no help at all.

It's not in my interest to help.

I hate you all.

I hate everyone named Martin ever.

Martin Van Buren? Dead to me.

Technically he's been dead to everyone
a REALLY long time

Not talking to you!

**3:07 p.m.**

I'm not going to survive.

I need you to call me and pretend you're
dying.

HE KEEPS SMILING AT HIS PHONE.

I can't do this.

Maybe I should choke on the pizza when it gets here.

MY DAD IS ORDERING APPETIZERS.

This is never going to end.

At least he's not mentioning his grandfather. That'd be a conversation that never ended.

Great, he mentioned you guys play WoW.

And he's a Paladin too??? Well, there goes that conversation.

My dad's in love with him now.

AND . . . HE JUST INVITED HIM TO THE BARBECUE.

I GIVE UP.

**9:18 p.m.**

I know it's almost plug-in, but are you better now?

I am never going to be better again.

And I don't have to plug in till 10. I thought I told you that.

You're not using all caps

That's something.

When did this change?

I get an extra half hour in summer.

My parents are just too good to me.

So I'm not bothering you.

I don't know if I'd go that far . . .

Your sarcasm has gone into overdrive.

This must be worse than I thought.

I have to distract you so you don't run away and join the circus or something before tomorrow.

Ooh, that's not a terrible idea.

It IS a terrible idea.

Plus imagine how many real maniac clowns you'd meet in the circus.

Yes, but it wouldn't be THIS maniac clown.

Doesn't your family have a big giant party thing tomorrow?

Shouldn't this burrito clown be going to that instead?

Normally yes.

Not this year.

Why is my life the worst?

It's not.

It is.

You really didn't enjoy yourself even a little bit this weekend?

That's the worst part.

He's actually really nice.

And that's bad?

Like, he even laughs at my jokes.

At the right parts.

I can't deal.

So being nice and getting your jokes is bad???

THE

WORST

EVER

I really don't get it.

I can't hate him when he's like that.

You still want to?

I'm doing my best.

That seems . . .

Weird?

Short-sighted?

Petty?

Childish?

Yes. I am every one of those things and more.

How about extreme?

I thought I explained it to you, but you still don't understand.

I REALLY don't.

I can keep my best friend or be nice to this random, unimportant dude. It doesn't seem like much of a choice.

Are you going to be mean tomorrow?

No.

That's what's worse than the worst.

You had fun!

I knew it.

I did.

Does this mean you're reevaluating those random and unimportant labels?

What is with you Martins?

It's all a giant plot against you

Wearing you down one day at a time.

What about you? What'd you do this weekend?

Stuff.

Did you talk to anyone last night?

Of course

She was super smart

Knew everyone

Or at least pretended she did.

She?

Jealous?

No.

Do I know her?

If I knew you . . . you'd know her.

This is doing nothing to help my hatred of Martins.

Martins are not that bad.

I know.

I'm just . . .

???

Nothing. It's nothing.

I'm being ridiculous.

Tell me about this barbecue.

It's nothing big.

Just my dad cooking all the meat in the entire world and us trying to eat as much as we can.

And what we don't eat my mom will frantically try to send home with everyone.

Who wouldn't want to go to that???

I guess.

But my uncles will be there.

And that's bad.

Well, my mom's brother is. He's SOOOO embarrassing.

Like, fifteen-thousand Os.

And your other uncles?

Only one other uncle this time.

He's actually my dad's friend.

And my uncle's friend.

He's only five-thousand Os embarrassing.

Will your cousins be there?

Yeah, and my aunt.

Oooh, I hope the clown doesn't try to eat all the chicken wings.

My aunt might stab him with a fork.

Oh, wait, maybe I hope he does.

So violent!

It's every person for themselves here.

I make no apologies.

Yeah you do.

Okay, yeah, I apologize constantly.

But it would be funny.

Plus, if word of bloodshed got back to Sarah and Chloe, I could have a reasonable excuse.

Oh crap, Lexi's going to stop by.

What am I going to say to her?

The truth???

He followed me home like a burrito clown puppy?

I don't know if I'd put it that way.

You're right.

But they WILL hear about it.

SO???

Ugh, I don't know what's going to happen.

This is going to explode.

I just know it.

It won't explode

You're going to be fine.

No freaking out.

It's way too late for that.

I'm well into freaking out.

You're fine

I'm fine

This is all fine.

You say that.

But you are safe. Far away in cyberspace.

Trust the all-knowing Martin.

Trust?

HA!

No thank you.

This is going to turn out all right

I promise.

I hope so.

Still breathing?

You're not funny!

Everyone will be here in like two hours.

Well, except my cousins, they'll be here soon.

Why are they so special?

They're toddlers. They get to show up whenever they want.

But also there will absolutely be a nap this time, so they need to get here so we can feed them and then put them to bed.

Does everyone get a nap time or just them?

I wish.

I barely slept last night.

Is it really that bad?

No.

Yes.

No.

Not really.

I'm just . . .

What if Chloe finds out?

What if Sarah finds out?

What if Lexi tells them?

What if they all freak out?

Trust me

They won't.

What's that supposed to mean?

Nothing

Just don't freak and they won't freak and everything will be all right.

I wish I believed that.

Just breathe.

OK?

**2:11 p.m.**

He's not here yet.

Lexi is, though . . . with about a metric ton of cookies.

Oh, plus, turns out you're right.

I guess Sarah and Chloe are going to some church thing today and Gabe will be there.

He was at Chloe's party and they talked and one thing led to another or something and he and Chloe got together or are getting together or whatever.

Are you at that church thing? Could you figure out what's going on? See how safe I am?

No, wait, scratch that.

I agreed. You're my internet friend who wouldn't know these people and not someone I can use for my own ends.

Forget I said anything.

Ugh, the burrito clown is here.

Okay, gotta go have the world's most embarrassing family party.

Later.

**6:45 p.m.**

I SURVIVED!

You did!

Oh, are you back?

Yeah.

Are you going to see the fireworks?

Getting ready now.

Oh, that's cool.

Very not cool.

Step2 called

She'll be back Friday.

The timer for the explosion is now set.

I can hear the clock ticking in the background.

Okay, that sucks.

I'm sorry.

Don't be.

You helped me forget about it for a while.

And you're really not going to fireworks?

OMG! Why will no one leave me alone about that?

It's kinda weird.

I am not a fan of the explosions or gunpowder or anything.

But they're so pretty!

Not pretty enough.

They're not pretty like thunderstorms.

You like thunderstorms

But you don't like fireworks?

I trust nature more than people. What can I say?

Fair.

But still un-American.

Uh, no, it's not.

It's just not modern American.

I can guarantee you Benjamin Franklin would be on my side about going out and blowing things up.

You think so?

He suggested the turkey over the bald eagle.

One will mess you up and the other will steal from you.

Except bald eagles are majestic like fireworks.

They're carrion birds.

Turkeys are hardcore.

And explosions are unnecessarily dangerous.

If you say so.

I do.

You realize you're talking about a dude who flew a kite in a thunderstorm in hopes of electrocuting himself.

Oh dear sweet boy, I bet you believe George Washington really cut down a cherry tree too.

He didn't?

Nope.

You need to stop reading your news feed. It's teaching you bad things.

It's teaching me TRUE things. That's more important.

This is positively un-American.

If the truth is un-American, I don't want to be right.

Wait, that came out wrong.

Pinko commie.

Am not!

I like the free market just fine.

Really?

Okay, I like a reasonably supervised market based on free market principles.

That doesn't even make sense.

See! American once more!

I'm glad you're feeling better

But I have to go.

My mother wants a REALLY good spot

And my father's already whining

And I'm reasonably sure they're going to trip the wrong wire well before Step2 even gets here.

I'm sorry.

I'm used to it.

That's why I'm sorry.

You'll be here if I need to vent?

Always.

Plus, I don't have to plug in until late. Holiday bonus.

Then you'll get to hear all about the explosions.

Ew.

Of the parental variety.

Even worse.

But, yes, I'll hear about them.

Because you put up with all my drama.

My mother's screaming up the stairs now

Later.

Don't lose a finger!

**11:35 p.m.**

Still allowed near your phone?

Yes, we're watching action movies to drown out the fireworks.

They've been over for hours.

Well, we're not done watching Nicolas Cage.

Nicolas Cage?

Classic movie night.

Can you talk?

Uh-oh.

What happened?

Nothing that wasn't expected.

You okay?

It's not like any of it is a surprise.

They're already screaming at each other

We barely made it out of the field before they started

And they didn't stop the whole drive to my mother's.

Is that where you are? Her place?

I'm at my father's

It'll be easier here

At least until Friday.

When your stepmom comes back?

Yeah

Then the timer starts all over again.

Well, I'll clean out my closet.

What would your family think of a strange boy living in your closet?

Well . . .

I would have said they'd freak out.

But after this afternoon, I'm more worried they'd like you even more than the clown and never let you leave.

My mom wouldn't let you leave anyway.

She's got a thing about kids going through divorces.

???

When my grandparents got divorced, one of her friends took her in for a while.

But she was in college and it was just for a summer.

But really, I guess they helped her a ton and she always likes doing what other people did for her.

That seems . . .

Weird?

Nice

Like super nice

But I shouldn't be surprised.

My parents are surprisingly nice.

Unless you break their stuff.

Especially do NOT break my mom's stuff.

Good thing you broke your father's garage door.

No kidding.

It's the worst when she's disappointed.

It fills the whole house.

Steals all the air.

You're right

Angry is easier.

My mother screaming at my father will go away.

Her disappointment in him NEVER will.

Yes, but I still wouldn't trade my parents for anything.

I don't know if I'd get any better.

I might trade mine for yours

But I still like mine.

Separately that is

VERY VERY separately.

Yeah, I guess.

Still sucks.

Still sucks.

You gonna be okay?

Probably.

Is it time?

Mom would let me stay up for this.

Really?

Of course. Soft spot, remember?

You should sleep

I'll watch some TV or something.

No PvP?

Not tonight

There's a new show I want to check out.

Okay, well, have fun.

Good night, Haley.

How are you doing?

Fine

Why?

Just checking in after last night.

Yeah fine.

I'm working.

Well, waiting.

I'm getting ready for work.

This early?

On a Tuesday?

Yeah, shifts changed around. This is what was left.

I'm on Tues and Thurs this month.

???

I get whatever no one else wants.

Plus, the new lady can do more hours after school starts.

That's not fair.

I'm cool with only a few hours a week. Better than nothing.

I guess.

She's a vet and has a kid and is going to school at the same time. She can get the sweet overnight pay if she gets fully trained on the deli stuff this summer, which I SO can't.

Vet as in veterinarian?

No, Afghanistan.

That's cool.

Yeah, except for it not being cool at all.

Gotta go

I'm being summoned.

**5:07 p.m.**

Why is the last hour of work always THE LONGEST?

Are you STILL working???

No, I just got home.

But I've been trying to message that to you with my brain for the last hour.

Sorry I didn't get it until now.

No?

Well, I'll work on that.

Psychic communication.

Because texting is just not fast enough.

I'm actually afraid you might achieve it.

You're still afraid of menopause?

STOP SAYING THAT WORD!

OMG, really?

Childish much?

We have to listen to you guys go on and on about erectile dysfunction.

I have never once in my entire life gone ON AND ON about erectile dysfunction.

You know what I mean.

Still.

Okay, fair.

I hope your day went well

Other than the boring last hour of course.

Yeah, it did.

Anything exciting?

Other than seeing the burrito clown for the fourth day in a row?

Nope.

And that counts as exciting?

Only if you're excited by burritos.

Wait.

Don't answer that.

Are you NOT excited by burritos?

UGH! I knew that was the wrong way to say that.

It wasn't exciting.

He just bought a burrito.

And yet you felt it was worth mentioning.

Okay, so we talked a little about Orphan Black.

Not a big deal.

He has come to understand the magic of Felix and, like all of us, needed an outlet for those feelings.

This sounds . . .

Weird?

Friendly.

Don't make me declare war on Martin-kind again.

Don't you need Congress for that?

Let me tell you the things I DON'T need Congress to decide I can or cannot do.

No, never mind that would take too long.

But your hatred of Martins is wavering?

Well, I'm not quite ready to forgive Van Buren for supporting slavery.

You've got to give him some credit for the Petticoat Affair.

You must have gotten a 5 on your AP test.

Oh right!

That's today!

You haven't checked?

Why are you talking to me?!

Shh . . . logging in.

I got a 4.

And a 3 in Chem.

And a 4 in Lang Comp.

You got a 3 in Chem???

I got 4.

I don't test well in science, remember?

Got a 3 in Calc so there's that.

What'd you get in US?

4 like you.

Despite picking the Articles of Confederation over Nixon?

I forgot about that!!!

You forgot why we started talking in the first place?

Washed my failure from my memory.

How'd you do in Lang Comp?

. . . 5

WHAT?

That's amazing! How'd you get a 5?

Don't know.

Doesn't that make you some kind of superstar?

No . . . I just have a 5.

Doesn't matter.

Shut up.

Don't be jealous

You're going to skip undergrad entirely and go straight into a PhD program.

Wait, why would I be jealous?

People get weird about stuff like this.

I'm impressed by you. This is impressed.

Is impressed weird?

Sorta

Don't know.

Okay, what's up?

Everyone at school gets so competitive.

True. It's a gifted and talented program.

Might as well call it Hunger Grades.

Exactly.

And yet you don't like telling people you're amazing at a thing they want to do well?

Are you afraid they'll worship you more?

Well, no.

You're afraid they'll think you're a nerd?

. . .

OMG! We go to a nerd school!

You would be their king.

I don't want to be their king.

You're already their king!

Okay, co-king. Whatever.

DEFINITELY don't want that.

Well, I'm proud of you.

Even though you did better than me and you didn't talk to me even once before taking the test.

Not true.

US History test was Friday

Lang Comp wasn't till Wednesday.

But I gotta go

I'm already running late.

Oh, have fun.

At our church baseball league???

It'll be a laugh riot.

Oh, well, break a leg.

That's theater.

Yeah, I've got nothing for sportsball, sorry.

**9:07 p.m.**

Are you still freaking out?

???

Your test.

Did your parents freak out?

They congratulated me.

That's it?

My mom wanted a party.

For two 4s and a 3?

Low standards.

After the whole Bio thing they said I could stop AP science, but I wanted to try Chem and it worked out better.

I never considered that.

Lowered expectations?

Any expectations at all.

My mother's disappointed in my Calc score.

What?!? Why?

Ridiculous.

She doesn't understand how hard it was.

English is easier.

Even being in AB your junior year is impressive.

Your mom's wrong. You did awesome.

I did like half as good as you.

We did the same on US.

Yeah, well, average it out.

You're like twice as smart as me.

Ridiculous.

But you're probably right.

I blame the biased school system.

You should just assume I know everything. Safer.

You're feeling good about yourself.

I got two 4s and a 3! That's like $10K less at college right there.

I'm the queen of the world!

You've got gender bias and a trust fund on your side, so there's almost no pressure involved.

Clearly taking four AP courses means nothing.

Fine, Your Majesty.

We're both smart.

Good you see that.

As you can tell, I can't talk to people who aren't smart.

They freak out and run away.

I haven't run away.

Well, you're odd.

Not as odd as you.

True. You wish you could be this odd.

Sometimes

Yeah.

Oh stop being serious.

Do you have any candy in the house?

Step2 left behind some gluten-free cookies.

THAT's sad.

Tell me about it.

Okay, tomorrow buy yourself a treat.

Something sugary and fatty and horrible.

And eat all of it and tell yourself it's from me.

I can do that.

Good.

It's time for you to go.

Yeah. Just about.

You good for real?

Am now.

No

I will be.

No pouting over being nearly as smart as I am.

Not that

Just thank you.

For being weird?

For being you.

Well, I'd suck worse at being anyone else.

No . . .

This is just the first time I had someone to talk to about all this.

You had Jack and your cousin.

Not really.

Yeah I had them

But not to talk to

Just to be around.

You don't talk about stuff?

Not like this.

What about your girlfriends?

Those were nothing like this.

Oh, right, I guess I'm your first girl-who-is-a-friend rather than girlfriend.

No

Never mind.

No, I get it.

Don't get all sappy. Just go pwn some n00bs in PvP.

No one says that anymore.

My parents still do.

Your parents are old-school nerds.

DON'T I KNOW IT!

Good night, supergenius Martin.

Good night, Your Majesty.

What do you do on your days off?

> Uh, what?

I'm sitting here at lunch and I realized I have no idea what you do on your days off.

> Well, stuff.

What are you doing now?

> Reading.

I guess I should have expected that.

Your news feed?

> No, actually.

> A book.

Something deep?

> Nope.

Educational?

> Double nope.

> It is fluffy. And silly and pointless, and I love it.

Like Pride and Prejudice?

> NO!

> I told you.

I don't understand.

It's just a book. It came out like a year or two ago. So not a classic. Not even an instant classic.

It has no empirical value except I enjoy it.

You're not bettering yourself as a person?

Well, sorta.

I can't freak out about where I'm going to go to college while I'm worrying about whether or not these two are ever going to kiss.

Is that something you often worry about?

College?

And kissing

Yes . . . No.

You'll get into college.

Yes, but will I get into the right college?

Will I regret it?

Will I be able to afford it?

No more talking about college

It's starting to freak ME out.

SEE!

So what about the kissing?

Ehn.

Too much?

No.

I don't know.

Yet you worry about imaginary people kissing.

Oh, yeah, other people kissing isn't remotely the same.

What about you?

I have almost no interest in imaginary people kissing.

No.

Do you read?

Not other than for school.

That's sad.

Not as sad as the end of my lunch break.

Good luck driving.

Good luck with the whole other people kissing thing.

If it doesn't happen, I'm so throwing this book in the trash.

Good plan.

**7:48 p.m.**

UGH!

Lexi is annoying me.

Hump Day problems or did she break up with Dylan again?

I REALLY don't want to take her stupid quiz.

???

If you don't, how will you know "Which Kardashian Should You Marry?"

You haven't seen? She's trying to get everyone to reveal where they fall on the Kinsey Scale.

??????

She thinks it's hilarious.

She's trying to out EVERYONE???

No. She's trying to show that we're all a little bit bi. Or whatever.

She's that sure?

I don't know. It's the stupidest test I've ever taken.

And that includes that AP Bio fiasco.

None of these questions make any sense.

It's not THAT complicated.

They're terrible.

My score keeps coming up X over and over again.

???

I don't know why anyone cares about a test written by horny academics in the '50s.

Is this freaking you out?

Like, I know sexuality is just a thing and people have it.

Or are it.

Or whatever.

But I'm pretty sure I only have just enough to make everything awkward.

But you like people?

I mean, yeah.

I LIKE tons of people, but it's kind of always too late to do anything about it.

Even if they may have liked me at first, they get the sister vibe and don't want anything else.

Jack doesn't get a sister vibe

I wish he did. I shouldn't have led him on . . .

Why did you go out with him in the first place?

Lexi thought we'd be good together or something. Sarah thought it would be "good for me" and went along.

They kept saying he liked me a lot.

I'd never had a boyfriend.

Then you guys just broke up out of the blue.

I couldn't do it.

I couldn't like him.

I thought it would be like all the other times and I'd start liking him if we spent time together.

But I never did.

You never wanted to kiss him?

I wanted to want to.

Really bad. It's not like I hadn't wanted to kiss someone before.

But it's never been the right person at the right time.

And Jack should have been that.

It would have made everyone happy. Him, Lexi, Sarah.

It would have even made me happy.

It would have been so much easier to want things the way everyone else does.

But you only made yourself miserable.

I get it.

Ha. Yeah, right.

No I do.

You have girls throwing themselves at you.

. . .

I made it weird again.

I'm a 2.

What?

Wait, like a Kinsey 2?

So, you're actually bi? Pan?

Bi.

I think . . .

It just fits better.

Oh.

You're freaked out.

No, actually.

I mean, sure, you surprised me.

Surprised?

Well, everything about you is just so . . .

Cishet?

Well . . . and mega allo about it.

Allo?

It's a thing.

Why do you do it?

???

Date half the school.

I don't DATE date them.

Girls are just easier.

Not EASIER easier but clearer. Girls are clearer that they like you.

Well, most of the time anyway.

Oh, well, yeah.

But I don't really date as much as you think.

I don't even date as much as other people think I do.

But I do like more than just girls.

I just want you to know I'm not making it up.

I believe you.

Wow

I've never just flat out said it like that.

To anyone??

Not anyone.

Oh.

Okay.

Now you're freaked.

No. I mean, a little. It's just . . .

You're freaked out by ME?

No! It's totally not that, I told you.

I just want to know . . . why me?

???

Why tell me? Why not your cousin or Jack.

You know, one of your friends?

You're my friend.

Well, sorta.

Definitely my friend

But you're not like THEM.

If you pull that "not like other girls" nonsense, I'm coming over there and shoving your phone down your throat.

You're not like my other FRIENDS.

When I talk to you I actually talk to you.

It's not just filling time.

You know who I am.

Well

You almost do.

I don't know who you are?

I wish you knew who I was.

You have this version of me in your brain that's so far from reality

Someday I'll get past it.

But I don't think you're ready yet.

Oh, okay.

So this is what?

A test?

A starting point.

Huh?

You still there?

Yeah, it's almost time.

I know.

What are you going to tell Lexi?

Nothing!!!

Wait, you mean the quiz?

I don't know.

Are you going to do it?

I don't know.

It's cool you're bi, you know.

It's cool you're so careful.

That's what you think?

Yup.

It's very you.

What? Weird?

No. You think about everything

Even being attracted to someone.

Well, you've got a point there.

I do think everything to death.

You think about it enough.

I think about it to death.

Trust me.

Always.

Weirdo.

Yup!

Good night, Martin, who potentially likes anybody.

Good night, Haley, who only likes people if they really deserve it.

Ugh.

Sleep tight!

Are we good?

What?

Yeah.

Why wouldn't we be?

Just checking. Last night was . . .

Not touching this one.

A lot?

Oh, yeah, I guess.

No, it was fine.

I'm getting ready for work.

I figured

As I said . . . I wanted to check.

Shouldn't you be driving somewhere?

Now is waiting time.

Later is driving time.

Oh, okay.

OK . . . so . . . have a good day at work.

Thanks.

Thought a lot about last night and I get why the whole Kinsey thing bugged you.

Don't say it like that.

Say what like what?

Thinking about last night?

???

It's just . . .

Weird?

Yeah.

What about it?

I don't know.

You don't think about me?

Well, no.

I mean, yeah.

I mean, I do.

But when you say it, it sounds . . .

Weird.

Right.

It's not weird.

I know, but—UGH.

Don't mind me.

I'm just tired.

Bad day?

No, actually.

Well, maybe.

"Strange" really is the best word for it.

???

Because it wasn't bad.

You're saying it should have been bad but wasn't?

Yeah, exactly.

So things that used to bother you about your job aren't?

I suppose.

What were you saying about Kinsey?

I see why it bothered you.

It's like attraction is on or off

Not all the stuff in between.

Right. Yeah. Exactly.

I can't lump all guys into a pile and say I'm attracted to them.

Same for girls.

Or anyone.

Yeah I think I get that part.

What?

It's not about everybody and making a decision.

Sometimes someone sneaks up on you and becomes something more.

EXACTLY.

It's kinda what it's like for me

With guys.

I USUALLY know right away if I like a girl or not.

Usually?

Sometimes they sneak up on me.

I don't like MOST guys right away.

I don't like most at all.

Like you . . . I can't like Jack.

Unlike you . . . I don't think he wants me to.

If you're trying to make me feel better . . .

I'm not.

There's got to be this thing

Oh, yeah, I get it.

Like a spark. But, ugh, I hate that term, you know, just like someone flipped a switch.

Like I'm just going along and realize I can see one person differently.

And once it's there . . . it's way bigger than the other kind of liking someone.

And this happens with guys?

Mostly. If it was about intensity like you said . . . I'd probably be more of a 4.

So it's some girls too.

One girl

It's happened with one girl.

Oh.

Was she particularly manly?

Definitely not.

Just skipped the spark

Way more like a dimmer switch.

Oh, okay. That's a good one.

Is there something wrong with her?

She's just special.

How about you?

Is it a dimmer switch for you?

I don't know.

I think I have a spark.

But it's with the person inside the skin more than the skin itself.

But I'm pretty sure if the options weren't so terrible I'd be a 1 at most.

Maybe I haven't met the right girl's soul or whatever.

But I don't get that feeling everyone else describes as love or even lust until I've really gotten to know someone.

Which is what screws everything up.

???

Either every guy I've ever started to like doesn't know or, more likely, doesn't care.

That's happened to you too?

Yeah, a couple of times.

So I let imaginary characters have crushes for me.

Hence all the reading.

Exactly!

That's sad.

Ugh, now you think I'm pathetic.

Not pathetic.

Just . . .

Weird?

You deserve better.

I'm sorry guys suck.

They don't suck.

They're just motivated more by sparks than I am.

It's cool.

No. That's not it.

It's not cool, but I've gotten better at being okay about it . . . sometimes.

That's very mature of you.

I know, right?

What about you?

???

Your guy thing? Does it make stuff complicated?

It has a couple times.

Really?

No, don't answer that.

???

I don't want to pry.

Don't worry you don't know these guys.

Oh? Really?

Then you could tell me if you wanted.

They were both at summer camp.

You mean the infamous church camp?

AWKWARD.

You have CLEARLY never been to summer camp.

Not a church one.

It's worse than normal camps.

The first guy was SUPER cute and super confusing.

Oh, really?

We shared a cabin

He was from like Wisconsin or something.

You don't even remember?

Do you remember his name?

I do but I'm not telling you.

Fine.

I deserve that.

Don't even think of posting this as some kind of fic.

Would I do that?

You wouldn't.

But no sexualizing my sexual awakening.

Trust me, that would never happen.

Not patronizing it either.

BAH! FINE!

I'm sure it was adorable.

Did anything happen?

I'm not telling you that part right now.

Fine, I deserve that too.

Urgh, I have to go.

We're eating.

This late???

Yeah, family time.

Speaking of, you're back at your mom's tomorrow?

Step2's flight arrives at 10 a.m. HUZZAH!

I'm sorry.

Don't be

I'll probably get at least THREE ice cream trips out of the deal.

Really?

Last time it was ten but I was thirteen so more ice cream inclined.

You're not ice cream inclined now?

I don't think they'll pander to it as much.

Parents.

Tell me about it.

## FRIDAY, JULY 8
### 12:08 p.m.

I don't want to work today.

I don't have to work today.

More imaginary people kissing?

Yes, but watching not reading.

???

Catching up on my dramas.

Shakespearean?

Korean.

I'm catching up on MY job sites.

Pretty sure I'm going to hit them all before the day is over.

You've already been to Europe once.

What more can you ask from the universe?

Are YOU going on a vacation this summer?

Sorta.

???

Yeah, we're going to another con—Gen Con in August.

???

Google it.

Seriously, how nerdy are you?

The nerdiest person you know.

Is that like this weekend's con?

No, this is way more about gaming.

What do you there? Raid?

No, it's more for tabletop than video.

That and swear at my phone because it has zero service despite us being in downtown Indy.

What's your poison?

Mostly board games, but there's some cool other stuff.

A bunch of authors go.

Kissing book authors?

No, the kind of SFF authors that would go to a gaming convention.

That makes more sense.

It's a kind of Mom-and-Dad thing more than a me thing.

That many people doesn't seem very vacation-esque.

Tell me about it.

There are so many people I can barely even Google anything while I'm there.

It's not my favorite, but I guess it's fun.

It's kind of tradition.

Plus, we drive.

You drive ALL the way there? That's got to take a whole day!

About eleven hours.

That seems . . .

Weird?

Excessive?

"Excessive" is the perfect word.

It's not bad.

This is why headphones were invented.

Plus, all the burritos a girl can eat.

You're into burritos now?

Gas station stuff is growing on me.

Have you ever been on a road trip?

No . . . thank all that is holy.

Oh, too good for the open road?

Too busy.

We fly

Everywhere.

Time is money.

Mostly I get dragged on business trips anyway.

Even with your mom?

My mother doesn't vacation

She works.

Okay, there's no way to ask this that's not totally insulting.

Or vaguely misogynistic.

???

Does she need to?

Not even a little bit.

If my father didn't have enough to keep her comfortable, my grandfather would happily give it to her.

So why does she work so much?

She likes to.

Ever since the divorce

Well, three years after the divorce.

One month after my father announced his engagement to Step1 to be precise.

She just woke up and decided she was done with the Munroes.

She used their money to put herself through school.

Now even when she's not at work she works.

How does she work not at work?

She's a staff accountant who does taxes on the side.

All year long?

Corporate taxes

They never stop.

Oh, really?

They slow down but she ALWAYS finds something to do.

That's how she found CHUCK.

I'm sorry.

I'm used to it.

I'm even more sorry.

No being sorry!!!

Oh, sorry.

I'm done now.

Back to the intern grind.

Godspeed.

I don't know how to say goodbye in Korean.

Good!

**5:38 p.m.**

You doing okay?

**7:18 p.m.**

I'm on a sugar high.

She really took you for more ice cream?

My mother firmly believes in sticking with what she knows

As evidenced by the fact that she's now back with CHUCK.

Oh.

Is that good or bad?

It's better than obsessing about my father.

I suppose.

Plus CHUCK got me a drone.

I'm not going to complain about that.

Drone? Airstrike or Peeping Tom?

I prefer to think of it as aerial reconnaissance.

Just so long as you don't use it to look in windows I'm okay.

I would NEVER do such a thing.

I'm trusted to "be the man of the house."

Ugh, does he think you're twelve?

He thinks he can win points by bonding with me

Which is better than how he wins points with my mother.

I don't have to go to their fancy meal this time.

So, what? Are you home alone?

Amped up on chocolate and banana and let loose into the world.

So not at home.

I'm at Jack's playing Xbox.

Oh.

Are you stomping him?

You know it.

I'll leave you alone, then.

Nah. Il's finishing him off right now.

Really?

Really.
You still there?

Nope.

I've died of embarrassment.

???

No reason.

Afraid I'm going to say something?

Yes.

No.

Maybe not on purpose.

Trust me.

Please say your phone is locked.

Fingerprint.

Ugh.

???

They could use your finger to unlock the phone.

Paranoid much?

Yes.

Horribly paranoid.

And not wrong.

And if they ask who you're talking to, say your friend from the internet.

What should I say this internet friend's name is?

Francis.

You can say I'm Canadian.

And a boy.

A BOY named Francis?

Yes, French Canadian.

I'm from Quebec and I put mayonnaise on everything.

Eww.

You do NOT hate mayo.

On everything???

Especially french fries.

THAT'S SO WRONG!!!!

You're not going to gross me out so I leave you alone again are you?

Are you????????

Thinking about it.

Too late I'm running away.

Night, Francis.

Good night, random stranger from the internet.

Okay, I'm going over to Sarah's, so don't message me.

???

They'll ask questions.

It'll get awkward.

They?

Lexi, Sarah, and Chloe.

Chloe again?

It's Sarah's birthday.

Oh right.

Yeah, so . . . all-night party.

I've saved you in my phone under Francis just in case.

So I'm only allowed to message you about hockey and maple leaves.

And Bieber.

Bieber???

He's Canadian.

Right . . .

Are you sure we're not at war with them?

You can talk about Trudeau too.

Everyone thinks he's dreamy.

Not my father.

Ah, yes, progressive social programs don't always go with big money.

My grandmother adores him

As does my grandfather.

His wife is on some board with my grandmother.

She does do a lot of charity work.

As does my grandmother.

How progressive.

I'm not touching that one.

Good job, Francis.

If you need me . . . I'll be here with my poutine and pancakes.

Ew.

Yeah. Regretting that one.

As you should.

You're not awake, are you?

Bonsoir, eh?

You don't have to be Francis. They're all asleep.

I guess you're not plugged in because you're not home.

Yeah.

Something like that.

???

Everything was just wrong.

???

I think Sarah has a crush on someone new.

But I only know this based on something Chloe said. Which means Chloe knows, but Lexi and I don't.

Mature.

Chloe wants us to know she knows, but not know who so we can't be in on it.

How Chloe of her.

Tell me about it.

Are you jealous?

Uncomfortable.

???

The entire night became about kissing and hooking up and double entendres and—UGH.

Plus, Lexi started implying that I had my own crush.

Anyone I know???

It was so stupid. Every time she mentioned it, Chloe would go on and on about Gabe and how amazing and sweet he is and how soon Sarah will be in the same situation.

Sounds painful.

It's just ridiculous.

I had to hear how they made out during fireworks.

It was sooooooooooooooooooooo romantic.

I nearly died from how sweet it was.

We all did.

This party could have taken a tragic turn.

Well, that explains why Gabe wasn't a total jerk at the game.

The game?

Church baseball league.

Oh, right. Tuesdays?

You DO pay attention to me!

Sometimes.

We also practice on Sunday nights.

Oh, trust me, I know that now too.

Are you any good?

Kinda.

They're going.

???

Sarah and Chloe. Which means Sarah's new guy is probably on your team.

It's all so ridiculous.

The entire world will be fine if we're not all paired up like breeding stock.

There's more to life than that.

Was it that bad?

You know Lexi's still dating Dylan.

It's good your hard work wasn't in vain.

It's not normally this bad. Normally we watch movies and Lexi will have some new craft project hobby thing she wants to get us all into.

One time we knitted and watched all the Twilight movies.

But you weren't talking about anybody?

Uh, no.

Not even Francis??

Ha! How cliché!

Yes, I'm totally in love with Francis. He's from Montreal. You wouldn't know him.

He's rich and good-looking.

Smells bookstores for me.

He's so perfect he even laughs at all my jokes.

Not all your jokes

Imaginary boyfriends do!

God, they'd laugh at me so hard.

It doesn't have to be Francis from Canada.

Plus, Lexi wouldn't believe me.

She kept implying things.

???

Just ridiculous stuff.

So what did you do?

Nothing.

Sat there like a lump.

Pretended to laugh.

That sucks.

Yeah.

Girls are complicated

Guys have it so much easier.

Yeah, you can play Xbox and ignore your feelings.

Exactly!!!

I wish I were playing Xbox.

I could handle a classic fighting game right now.

Mortal Kombat?

More like Soulcalibur.

Have you played the new one yet?

A little. I'm not actually good, but it definitely beats taking sex quizzes online.

What did you do?

What I always do:

Lied.

Guessed.

Looked like a weirdo.

I can't imagine you looking like a weirdo.

You're not terribly creative.

You love it.

You look like a weirdo.

Feeling better?

Yeah.

I should probably sleep.

Oh, sorry.

I didn't mean to keep you up.

You're not

I should sleep anyway

Church . . . remember?

Oh, right.

Well . . .

Sleep tight.

Don't let them get to you

You're fine just the way you are.

Whatever.

Unless you put mayo on your fries and then I take it back.

But it's so yummy!

Now who's the weirdo?????

Still you!

Good night, Francis.

**3:28 p.m.**

I'm so sorry about today . . .

I didn't think she'd make us all go to church.

I would have warned you but there wasn't time and her parents made us give them our phones before we left.

**4:18 p.m.**

It wasn't a big deal.

I made everything awkward.

I didn't think real life would be so strange.

I tried to apologize, but I never really had the chance.

It was fine.

It was weird.

I made it weird.

Church isn't supposed to be weird.

See this is how I know you weren't lying when you said you've never actually been to church before.

It's weird ALL THE TIME.

Oh.

But we were all sitting together there in that group on the benches.

And then we went to lunch with like EVERYBODY.

And I was wearing jeans.

Why was I wearing jeans?

Jeans were fine

Other people were wearing jeans.

Yeah, GUYS. The girls were wearing DRESSES.

It wasn't a big deal.

It was a big deal.

I mean, it's not like I was introduced to your grandfather.

OH WAIT . . . I WAS!

He thought you were sweet.

OMG.

Wearing jeans, at a church, with a financial genius, near what I presume were your parents or stepparents or whatever.

Why did that clown drag me over there like that? I could have gotten away with being a lump in the corner the whole day.

No wonder you didn't talk to me.

I wouldn't talk to me either.

You weren't that bad.

He kept explaining stuff to me like I was a child.

Like, yes, I've seen a cross before. I understand the implications.

I know you've seen a cross before

It was just a conversation.

He must think I'm an idiot.

And then Jack.

What was THAT about? Did the clown mess up in 3v3 or something?

I can't believe I had to sit still for an hour between both of them when they were fighting.

I thought I was going to die.

You weren't sitting still for an hour.

Oh yes, the CHANTING!!!!!!!

That wasn't awkward AT ALL.

The recitation.

And the singing? Thankfully my mom likes to sing hymns now and then.

At least I knew some of the melodies.

You were fine.

I'm just glad you're better at this than I am.

???

Pretending like you don't know me.

It was the only way I kept from embarrassing you the way I did that clown.

You didn't embarrass me.

I embarrassed everyone.

I kept calling your grandfather Martin the First.

You were clarifying

He liked it.

It was weird.

I was weird.

You were perfect.

Don't freak out.

But what about you?

What about me???

Well, if it's permissible to acknowledge we saw each other in real life, what were you and Sarah whispering about before?

???

In church.

In the pews or whatever.

I don't know what you're talking about.

Don't you remember? When that old lady shushed you guys??

. . .

Fine. Be like that.

You are of no use to me!

FRANCIS.

You're right

I'm not

Gotta go drink my bagged milk

That's not a thing.

Is!!! But I DO have to go

Practice.

Okay, well, I'll be here replaying every moment of the day in my head.

Let me know if you finally figure anything out.

Mostly just more ways to be embarrassed.

There's definitely more to figure out than that.

Whatever, just leave, heartless Canuck.

God save the Queen!

I spend WAY TOO MUCH of my life staring out windshields.

Imagine if you were a trucker.

Good point.

I spent WAY TOO MUCH of my summer looking out windshields.

It's better than staring at the same four walls most of the time.

This is where we differ.

Oh.

I'll bet.

You don't even have the same four walls to stare at. Do you?

Don't get me wrong . . . I LIKE both my rooms.

My parents made sure of that.

Are they all tricked out? Like gaming systems everywhere?

My father yes. My mother no.

My father's whole house is wall-to-wall toys.

Anything second gen goes into my room.

Your life sucks.

Doesn't it?

My mother barely lets me have a computer.

What? With an old dial-up and a two-color monitor?

Still a top-of-the-line gaming system

But that's it

Just a computer.

No Xbox

PS4

ANYTHING.

No tablet?

Well

I have my tablet AND phone

But I always have those.

Obviously.

You're making fun of me

Little bit.

I don't need any of your middle-class lip.

Yeah, you do . . .

But I can't too much.

I have an old Xbox, live in a house with five computers, and have my own smartphone.

You're not bad off either.

Yeah, I'm really not.

That's why I feel bad about freaking out sometimes.

???

Well, I don't have anything wrong with my life.

I mean, my parents are reasonable.

Your parents are awesome.

Reasonable.

They take care of me and give me everything I need.

But they're constantly annoying.

And then there's my friends . . .

What happened with your "friends"?

Lexi asked me to come over and help her with a project.

I'm not sure I should ever leave the house again.

???

She wants my help painting a mural in her bedroom.

I didn't know you are artistic.

I'm not.

She just wants me to sit there and talk to her while she paints.

You should go.

I should. But I just can't.

There's too much in my head.

What are you up to instead? More kissing books?

No, helping my mom with a project.

She kinda hates our bathroom.

So I'm organizing the linen closet.

Sounds . . .

Weird?

Boring?

Obsessive?

Let's go with "boring."

I am sorting things by kind and putting them in baskets and labeling the baskets.

Obsessive it is!

But in a good way

Sounds kinda helpful.

It will be. It has to be.

If I never leave the house again, at least I'll know where to find the tweezers.

Personal hygiene bucket?

. . . the first aid bucket.

That makes sense.

You think I should put them in personal hygiene.

First aid but hang them off the side?

I should have thought of that.

I'm going to screw this up too.

I don't know what I'm going to do with you.

Nothing to do, really.

I'll think of something.

Weirdo.

Your fault.

Whatever.

Lunch is over.

Good luck with your sorting.

Good luck with your windshield!

Thanks!

### 6:57 p.m.

How goes the bathroom?

For two women who never paint our nails, we sure do own a lot of nail polish.

Why don't you paint your nails?

Not a lot of point.

It's a lot of work for very little benefit.

I can see that

I like the idea of painted nails more than the real thing.

My mom likes them, but she says she likes them better when they flake off.

???

She used to be goth back in the day.

Explains SO much.

Yeah, but she says she was a terrible one. But still, she tells stories about being a club kid in DC the first time goth was a thing.

She was also a pitiful club kid.

She was the sober one who used to babysit everyone else.

If it were anyone else . . . I wouldn't believe it.

Right?

Can't you just see her? Surrounded by the eternal ennui and still totally in control?

Downing acetaminophen at four to six hour intervals.

Hah! You remembered.

That's got to be it. Acetaminophen and an overactive responsibility complex.

Have you checked HER for a "so responsible it hurts" tattoo?

If she has one, it's not in any of the obvious places.

I'm leaving that alone.

At least she gives me a really good excuse if anyone tries to push drugs or alcohol on me.

"Thanks, but no, I'm so responsible it hurts."

Has that ever happened?

No, but I'm totally ready for the day it does.

I'm looking forward to witnessing it.

You'd be so lucky.

I'm bringing popcorn.

You get me.

It's for me to munch on while you destroy the peer pressure-er.

Yes, but when I'm done I'll have popcorn!

IF I save you any.

You would.

You sure of that?

You'd be too afraid not to.

True

Very true.

## TUESDAY, JULY 12
### 6:08 p.m.

Sorry I disappeared last night.

Mom started talking to me and next thing I knew it was plug-in.

### 6:20 p.m.

I figured.

I'll be slow

At the game.

You better not be in the outfield texting me.

I play third base.

Well, you better not be on your phone at third base—you'll get hit in the head with a ball.

We're at bat

I'm up in a bit.

Are you any good at batting?

I've hit the ball before.

So, no.

I'm not joining the school team.

No MBA or whatever?

Major League Baseball.

Oh, I should have remembered that.

I'm disappointed.

You should be.

Back after I strike out.

so youre even texting him at the game??

Who is this?

his dear friend jack

who is this??

No one you know.

Should you be touching your friend's phone?

why not?? he touches plenty of my stuff

How about you lock his phone up and put it away?

he has you saved as HER??????

why are you keeping this all a big secret

Stop being a jerk.

oh come on . . . prove me right

No. Jack, what's wrong with you?

just that im always right

You're just gossip-mongering.

i don't want him hurt

You're the one hurting your friend, not me.

youll understand if i don't trust you

I don't know why you wouldn't.

pretty sure you do

You don't know me and I don't know you, so I don't see why you're making a big deal out of this.

don't think so

can always check the history

bet it wouldnt take much to prove youre the dangerous one

You can't and you won't.

I'm a total stranger from the internet.

And you're two poor life choices away from death.

you did not just threaten me over M

youve been flirting with him????

I'm not flirting with him.

We're just friends.

This is his cousin, Martin II 🙂

You are aware there's two of us 😉

Of course I know there's two of you.

Now put your cousin's phone down and walk away while I'm being nice.

Don't mind Jack he's a bit 🙃

Are you coming to Wade's party this weekend? 👽

I have no interest in public scrutiny.

Interesting . . . normally girls want to show off Munroes every chance they get 😌

Why are you being like this?

If my cousin is interested enough in you to talk to you this much, I don't see why I shouldn't be interested as well 😌

You're not remotely interested in me.

I'm a distraction because you're bored.

You're playing with me.

Admit it!

ME AGAIN!

The one time I get a base hit

Of course I was stuck out there.

I'm so sorry.

I SWEAR I locked my phone.

OMG.

I totally freaked.

I just kept talking to them.

I couldn't stop.

I'm sorry.

I hope I didn't make things weird.

Game's over.

I'M sorry. No reason for you to be.

You didn't do anything wrong.

I shouldn't have had my phone out.

No, don't be sorry.

Were you THAT freaked they'd figure out who you were?

No.

Yes.

I mean, not for myself.

I was more worried about you.

???

I don't know.

It's ridiculous.

I didn't want them to see all the stuff we talked about.

???

I mean . . . Jack's the worst. I don't want to have to hurt him.

Hurt him more you mean

I'd probably wimp out at the last minute, but I'd totally intend on hurting him.

No, for this I'd really do it.

You'd consider hurting your ex for me?

UGH! Don't call him that.

You make it sound like I'm promoting domestic violence.

Really, I'd probably just glare at him.

Your death rays?

You'd make him cry.

I know he'd cry.

You'd break his heart.

Wouldn't.

Would.

I think he still likes you.

UGH.

WHY DO YOU KEEP SAYING THAT?!?

Because it complicates everything.

Now I need to wash my brain out with soap.

At least you know where the soap is.

True. I labeled it.

Sorry if I freaked you out.

I'll be more careful.

No, I'm fine.

Well, not the Jack part.

You're hallucinating if you think he likes me.

Boys are simple.

Yeah, right. Your cousin isn't . . .

What was all that about?

It was nothing.

???

I was almost starting to rethink the clown's jerk status.

You were?

I mean, he still comes into the gas station.

I don't know if I told you that.

You've implied it.

We've started talking a little if it's slow.

Mostly he comes in during lunch, so it's not REALLY slow.

But then he was really nice to me on Sunday.

And after the con.

Now . . . I don't know.

I'm going to kill him.

No. Don't. I'll just poison his Slushee.

Thanks for the warning.

I wouldn't really do it.

I'd just think about it.

A lot.

One step forward

Two steps back.

This is why you're right. We have to stay internet friends.

...

I'm sorry I'm a freak.

I've gotta go though.

Sorry again about tonight.

Not as sorry as they're going to be.

So Step2 cleared out all her stuff and is moving back to the West Coast.

Oh no, I'm sorry.

It's fine.

Is your dad okay?

Fine

He's the one who exploded it

And he had a prenup.

That's . . .

Typical.

Well, no.

Not even close.

I mean, it's a sound decision for someone who's on his third marriage to someone he's in business with.

He's an idiot.

Is this going to ruin his company?

Both make too much money from it.

So what are you going to do?

I'll stay with him on weeknights

At my mother's on weekends.

Awkward dating will really begin that quickly?

It's already begun.

My mother

Remember?

Oh wow. Are there others?

Like does he revisit the backlist?

Doubt it

Step1 is already remarried and has a kid.

Even HE'S not going to break that up.

So he goes out and finds new people?

Just like that?

He's calling it his "triumphant return to the bachelor lifestyle."

But he'll find Step3 soon enough.

He won't try again with your mom?

CHUCK bought her a car

A Jag.

Says I can borrow it "if I'm good."

He what?

He wanted to buy me one too.

She talked him out of it.

Matching Jaguars? Isn't that going a little far?

That's what I thought

But I think he's serious.

About European sports cars?

About my mother.

Even though they broke up and she hooked up with her ex?

I think CHUCK being serious might have been WHY they broke up.

He said something about how this will do until she takes the ring.

So he proposed?

I don't know.

I don't really know anything.

Is it really that bad?

I mean, he's a little over the top, but he doesn't sound evil or anything.

I never thought of my mother having another husband.

She hasn't actually agreed to anything yet. Right?

Guess not.

Right, plus, you'll definitely get ice cream before it happens.

True

That helps.

Ice cream?

Knowing there will be some kind of warning.

Oh, yeah. Well, she kind of has a tell, doesn't she?

She totally does.

But what about you?

Shouldn't you be working on your bathroom project?

Taking a lunch break.

Is that allowed?

Who cares?

You're on lunch break, so I'm on lunch break.

So you're not still upset about last night?

What?

No.

I'm sorry about them

All of it.

You've already said that.

They ruined everything.

What could they ruin? It's not like either of them are a surprise.

That's who they are.

They always have been.

It's not who I am.

It's definitely not who I want you to THINK I am.

They don't mean anything.

Jack's Jack and your cousin . . .

I don't know about him anymore.

I was starting to think I did.

I knew this would happen.

I'm sorry.

You shouldn't blame yourself.

It's not that

I keep screwing this up.

It's not that big of a deal.

He screwed everything up . . . Like always.

I almost had it all figured out.

You're fine.

We're not fine.

I don't know if I can ever actually make this fine.

Oh.

I'm sorry.

It's not that.

ARGH!

There's stuff I have to tell you

But I'm kinda scared.

What would you be scared of?

You

You're just so you

All the time.

Weird.

No.

You don't get it.

I don't think you WANT to get it.

No, I do.

You could explain it to me.

Not yet

Not without ruining everything.

I still can't figure out how to do this without anyone getting hurt

I know you're going to hate me

I'm not going to hate you.

Whatever it is. It'll be all right.

I wish I could believe that.

Look they're calling me back to the office.

Okay.

**5:42 p.m.**

You feeling better?

Fine.

That earlier was nothing

Ignore it.

Family stuff got to me or something.

I'm sorry I'm so terrible about . . . those people you talk to in real life.

You're protective of your friends

Even when they don't deserve it.

It's kinda why I'm still talking to you.

Kinda?

Well . . .

You also don't need me to explain what I mean by things.

People ask you to explain stuff too?

All the time!!!

Words . . . metaphors . . . examples.

I just had to explain to a guy at my last job site "what a meme was."

OH YES! I KNOW! ALL THE TIME!

Like, guys, if you don't know what a phyllosilicate is, Google it. I do.

I can't believe they've made it this far in life without realizing they can search as fast as ask me.

Exactly.

**9:35 p.m.**

You really sure you're okay?

I don't want you to get upset again.

I decided I've got to do something about all this.

I just don't know how yet.

Yeah, I know how that goes.

Why do you talk to me?

What?

This again?

I KNOW why I talk to you.

I don't.

I told you.

I guess.

Why do YOU talk to ME?

Because.

You can do better than that.

It's almost time to plug in.

But it isn't.

Just one thing.

Please???

You won't laugh?

Probably not.

This does not instill confidence in me.

I won't laugh.

This is what I thought friendship is supposed to be like.

What do you mean?

I mean, I thought Sarah and Lexi and I were going to be friends forever.

And now Sarah wants to spend more time with Chloe than either of us.

And Lexi's only interested in the results of my ideal seduction technique quiz.

(The test literally said I have none. I know you're shocked.)

We used to do everything together. And now it's like we're strangers.

You know almost as much about me as they do and you haven't run away yet.

Right.

RIGHT!

Exactly.

You haven't run away yet.

Look, I really have to plug in.

I know.

You sure you're okay?

I'm better now.

Well, that's something.

Good night, friend.

Good night, weirdo.

Did you tell him something?

???

The burrito clown was being strange today.

Stranger.

Progressively more strange.

Did you say something to your cousin?

I told my cousin nothing about anything.

So you didn't talk to him about Tuesday?

???

After all that stuff I thought . . .

Never mind.

He was just being weird. As I said.

Weird?

He was really . . . nice . . . kept apologizing about stuff.

Like he knew I was mad at him.

And?

And what?

Do you still hate him?

I don't hate him.

After the con and the party I guess I stopped hating him for a second.

It's just all complicated.

But I guess I realized something just now.

???

He didn't know that was me.

I mean, you really could be talking to a French Canadian you met on the internet for all he knew.

And like I know he was being a jerk because it's his job.

Is he really THAT bad?

No, he's not.

But he really does think that whole bad-boy thing works.

You think it's a bad-boy act?

I mean, look at what happened with Sarah and then AGAIN with Chloe at prom.

That's not reality

Maybe not.

Maybe it's because he's so nice to girls we keep getting the wrong idea.

Making things into stuff he didn't mean.

Which isn't his fault, but it makes it REALLY hard to figure out what he's thinking.

Maybe the burrito clown hadn't met the right person.

Boys are so dumb sometimes.

As a boy I take offense at that.

Well, not you.

Well, okay, sometimes you.

But you're the good kind of dumb.

There's a "good kind"?

Yeah.

I'm afraid to ask.

You're the kind that makes me laugh.

I can handle that.

Good.

Can't crush your fragile male ego.

!!!

Hahahahahaha!

Fine . . . I'll let it go.

But . . .

Uh-oh.

Do you dislike him or not?

Dislike who?

The burrito clown

Martin Nathaniel Munroe II

The one who comes to visit you at work.

Oh.

Him.

No.

No.

I guess you could say I'm disappointed.

I can work with disappointed.

Why are you so invested in us getting along? Does he have to approve all your friends?

...

Weren't you just trying to convince me like a month ago you're not actually the same person?

As you say

It's complicated.

What are you up to tonight?

Nothing.

Well, sorta nothing.

Gotta catch up on my stories.

???

Yeah, so many good dramas. You have no idea.

More foreign television?

You make it sound so elitist.

This is my crap TV that I get from the other side of the world.

You're a crap TV snob?

YOU KNOW IT!

You're clearly in a mood now.

CLEARLY!

I will not keep you from your "stories."

You and your scare quotes.

Why? What are you doing?

I'm going to the complication's house.

Which one?

Har dee har har

Notice I manage not to insult your friends.

Lately . . .

So you do appreciate how hard I'm trying.

What are you doing when you go to this "complication's" house?

Per usual there will be many rousing games.

We MAY even go outside!

Are you really still trying to catch them all?

I worry about you some days.

I AM HIP AND WITH IT!

You're so very not.

Whatever.

I'm awesome.

THAT I can't argue with.

Or you'll get a face full of mayonnaise fries.

UGH!

No.

Go away!

HA! You're the worst French Canadian ever.

I'm starting to wonder if you even know what a French Canadian is.

You're just jealous that you don't know what good french fries taste like.

I thought you had better things to do.

Oh, right.

Yeah.

I totally do.

Birth secrets and undisclosed cancer diagnoses.

Cheerful.

It is!

Have fun!

You too!

And keep your phone locked!

Yes, ma'am.

Hey.

Lunchtime?

Yeah.

What are you eating?

The usual.

What's your usual?

Something I pick up nearby.

Cool.

Am I bothering you?

What?

No.

Sorry. No.

I was just eating.

I can leave you alone.

No, it's not that.

How did last night go?

???

Was it the three of you?

Just ll and me.

Really?

It happens.

How'd last night go for you?

Oh, it was fine.

I made it through most of my shows and then Lexi wanted to gossip.

???

Just the usual.

Am I going to Wade's party?

Do I want to know in excruciating detail how Dylan pissed her off most recently?

Who do I think Sarah is flirting with this time and how is it going?

What is Chloe's deal?

What am I up to and does it involve any of my customers?

Lexi's been getting too much sun this summer, I swear.

Has she developed a sudden interest in the gas service industry?

No, she's just got these theories about everything.

I was making a bad joke.

That was supposed to be a joke?

I said it was bad.

It was nonexistent.

No more jokes.

A fine rule.

I don't really have anything to say.

Just wanted to say hi.

Oh.

Okay.

So . . . hi.

I've hurt you with this no-joke thing, haven't I?

No, I really don't have much to say.

Yeah, me neither.

Maybe we've run out of stuff to talk about.

I doubt that.

You'll read of a new use for acetaminophen and we'll be back at it again.

I told you about that, didn't I?

You mean the existential crisis?

No, that it's also been found to be an effective tool for surviving heartbreak?

???

I guess they're finding that in low doses it numbs your empathy receptors.

So they're coming up with a ton of cool uses for it.

What are empathy receptors?

Uh, maybe that's not the right word.

Your empathy processors?

You mean taking too much acetaminophen could make you a serial killer or something?

I think if you take enough of it to do that, you'll have already blown out your liver anyway.

So it's got a fail-safe built in

That's something.

Yeah, morality is quite often a trade-off for your ability to process toxins.

I'll keep my morality AND my liver.

Good choice.

Very un–French Canadian of you.

I may start sending you articles about Montreal

It's an area of study you could benefit from.

I'm fine with my wildly inaccurate presumptions about the Québécois, THANK YOU VERY MUCH!

If you say so.

Just don't actually go there.

But, but, poutine!

You can get poutine here without causing a diplomatic incident.

It's because I don't know French, isn't it?

Not even a little bit.

OK maybe a little bit.

I see how this is.

I'm part French Canadian on my father's side, I'll have you know.

That doesn't make this any better!

I cannot win with you, can I?

You could if you tried something else.

Maybe, but later, my mom's calling.

**4:58 p.m.**

Glad that's over.

What? Work?

What'd you think?

With you? Could be anything.

No, not anything.

But it could be a lot of things.

True for you too.

Not today.

Today I'm nearly nothing.

That's rather nihilistic.

I suppose.

You OK???

Me?

Yeah, why?

You seem . . .

Weird?

Quiet.

Oh. Maybe.

Lexi got me thinking about stuff is all.

Uh-oh.

Is that a problem?

She freaked you out about something?

Like that's hard!

Ha.

You're not the only one.

Why, are you freaked?

Sorta.

Your family?

No.

Yes

No

Sorta.

Well, that cleared that up.

Sorry.

Does this have anything to do with a secret?

???

Just . . .

How'd you guess???

Told you I was thinking.

Really

Why do you ask that?

Really, it's nothing. You don't have to tell me. I was trying to be funny. Sorry for making it awkward.

My dad just came home, so I have to go.

OK.

**7:18 p.m.**

So are you going?

To Friday Funday?

It was canceled because of Wade's thing tomorrow.

I mean THAT.

You mean, am I going to Wade's thing???

Yeah.

Lexi thinks I should.

But you don't?

I don't know.

I usually feel lonelier around more people.

???

It goes with being the quiet one.

Someone would talk to you.

Right.

Awkward conversations about, what?

Music?

Why I'm not drinking?

Who I came with?

Why I'm not dancing?

How my flailing might have left a bruise after someone forced me to dance?

It won't be THAT bad.

It'll feel that bad.

I just thought

Maybe

You would come.

What? Why?

I wanted to talk to you about something

In person.

It's one of those conversations that would benefit from you being prepared it was going to happen.

You can't like come to work or something?

It's definitely not a conversation I want to have over burritos.

But shouted over dubstep is fine?

We'll talk outside.

Why can't we talk now?

Now works.

In person

I need to see you when I say this stuff

You need to see me

You deserve to have it said to your face.

Please. We NEVER talk in person.

There's a first time for everything.

Will you come?

Okay, fine.

But I can't guarantee I'll stay.

Stay long enough to talk

I said fine.

But this isn't really helping me prepare.
Is this a bad conversation?

???

Like, will I cry?

I hope not.

I hope you'll think it's a good thing.

Okay. So no mascara. Check.

???

If I'm going to a party, Lexi is going to insist
on dressing me, which includes makeup.

If I wear mascara, I'll look like a raccoon
when I cry.

Maybe no mascara.

So it is going to be bad?

I don't THINK so. But I don't know how much to prepare for.

You have to promise not to freak until I've explained everything.

I'm not going to freak on purpose.

Good.

You're being weird.

Am not.

A little bit.

You want to talk?

In person?

Kinda weird.

You're going to get the wrong ideas.

I promise, no ideas.

Okay, minimal ideas.

Minimal is the best I can ask for.

But I have to go

My father wants to lose at Rocket League

Car soccer?

You play car soccer?

No.

I dominate car soccer.

Figures.

# SATURDAY, JULY 16
## 3:26 p.m.

You're still coming?

Right???

Yes.

Dylan's picking Lexi and me up at my house after she helps me get ready.

Your request has made her month, even though she's convinced I'm going for some other totally ridiculous reason.

You're riding in the hoopty?!

Don't worry, I made sure to get my tetanus updated after the last time.

Why does he even still drive that thing?

It gets him from A to B.

What else does a car need to do?

Not destroy the environment single-handedly.

Okay, I mean, there's that.

But then he'd have to give up the sweet mural.

How would he get around without a unicorn rampant on the side?

How do you get around without one?

It like gets the girls or whatever.

True.

That's what you should ask your mom's boyfriend for.

Think he'd get me one?

I don't know, do those Porsche minivans come with unicorns?

Could you imagine the look on CHUCK's face?

Well, no, but I can kind of guess.

Might be worth it.

Oh man, I've given you ideas.

Always.

Are you really going to be safe in Dylan's piece of crap?

Yeah, this is not my first experience with shock-less conversion vans that are as old as my father.

It's THAT old???

I should pick you up.

Maybe you should just trust that I know what I'm doing.

Fine

Just

Be careful.

Now who's freaking?

Touché.

Are you here yet?

No. We're getting pancakes. Chocolate chip pancakes.

Whatever you have to say can wait until after chocolate chip pancakes.

Fine

I know what a bad idea it is to get between you and chocolate chip pancakes.

I can wait.

You really need to relax.

We won't be there until after 8.

Seriously???

Hey, I'm just the passenger.

Against my better judgment.

It's barely even 7.

Wade has a pool.

Oh great, a water hazard to avoid!

I should have picked you up

You're going to figure out some way to get out of coming.

I'm not.

I'm coming. I'm not even freaking.

But I'm pretty sure you may be.

Sarah's here.

You wouldn't be alone.

Is Sarah alone?

???

Just something Chloe implied the other day.

That'll have to wait until you get here.

I'll be there when I get there.

Gotta go, my pancakes are here.

**8:01 p.m.**

Where are you???

OMG, chill.

We're finding parking.

Good!

Meet me behind the pool house in fifteen.

Behind?

There's a little garden there.

Okay, fine.

I'll trust you this once.

Remember no matter who's back there you promised not to freak.

I don't remember making that promise.

Please trust me?

**8:25 p.m.**

Where are you???

**9:08 p.m.**

Are you OK???

Did something happen?

Jack said he saw you crying

Did you get hurt?

Did the fireworks freak you out???

I told Wade not to get those out.

Is that why you left before we had a chance to talk?

Talk to me

I'm sorry I wasn't there. I was helping Sarah with something.

**10:15 p.m.**

I'm fine.

It's nothing.

I just had to go.

Did something happen at home?

Are your parents all right?

Did something happen to your cousins?

Did you hurt yourself?

Everyone's fine.

I guess you could say I hurt myself.

Was it the hoopty?

No, nothing like that.

Look, I'm sorry I couldn't stick around for whatever you wanted to say to me.

I just couldn't.

Something happened.

Yeah.

But I DON'T want to talk about it.

So . . . Chloe and I got into a fight.

A big one.

I guess rumors are going around that make NO sense. And since they involved the clown she believed them.

She said she was trying to protect me from what happened to her, but I said she was being ridiculous.

I tried to explain, but she wouldn't listen.

She kept saying things are really complicated for Sarah right now and that's why she can't trust me anymore.

Chloe felt she needed to say something to me before I made it worse.

They're just burritos . . .

My PARENTS invited him to the barbecue.

HE sat by ME in church.

But that was only because she and Gabe took the last two seats in that row and I had to sit behind everybody.

He's the one practically stalking me and I'M the one she says is being a terrible friend to Sarah.

I didn't ask for any of this.

## 1:15 a.m.

Stalking you?

That's what you really think?

Haley?

Are you sleeping?

If not . . . can you talk to me?

## 8:04 a.m.

Please?

## 6:17 p.m.

Okay, I finally got to sleep, and I'm thinking a bit clearer.

I shouldn't have freaked out at you. This isn't your fault.

Not really.

You think this is stalking?

No . . .

Stalking is harsh.

Following.

Being everywhere.

You didn't seem to be as upset about it anymore.

It's just so complicated. She was saying so much stuff. Like the last couple of months have been a blur.

293

Everything was so confusing . . . him . . . you . . . Chloe . . . Sarah.

UGH. I want to talk to you.

But I can't.

I shouldn't.

Why not?

It's too meta.

Even for us.

???

So . . . I'm sorry.

But just . . . can whatever you wanted to say wait?

I need space.

I guess it has to now

I had just thought . . .

No

I didn't think.

I wanted this too bad

But it can wait

I can wait.

Thank you.

I'm sorry.

I'm sorry too.

# MONDAY, JULY 18
## 12:35 p.m.

Hi.

This is Francis.

Would you be willing to tell me wildly inaccurate facts about my culture while I eat lunch?

Uh.

Please? I don't have anyone to talk to while I consume these ketchup-flavored potato chips.

Ew, who would do such a thing?

Seriously?

Do you know NOTHING about Canada?

It shares a northern border with the United States?

Why did you even pick Canada?

Could have picked Korea and been way more convincing.

No one would have believed it if I suddenly had a guy friend in Korea.

They'd have called it wish fulfillment and made inappropriate yet legitimate jokes about fetishization.

Do you really think Lexi would ever accuse you of fetishization?

A girl can dream!

So does this mean you'll speak to this entirely unfetishizable Canadian?

Haley?

Do not make me start quoting Canadian facts at you.

We shouldn't be talking so much.

You clearly don't know that Canada has the largest landmass after Russia.

I'm not a good person to be friends with.

We also have more lakes than all other lakes in the world combined.

Really? Even Minnesota?

Ryan Reynolds is Canadian!

He is?

Where are you reading this?

Wait . . . do you really have a celebrity crush on him?

There are a surprisingly large number of websites that contain twenty-one facts about Canada.

Canadian clickbait?

. . .

But you made those potato chips up, right?

GOOGLE IT!

OMG. THIS IS DISGUSTING.

Ketchup Doritos?

WHO DOES THAT?

And YOU thought you needed to make up wildly inaccurate details about Canada in order to impress me?

These people are freaks.

I'm not claiming to be part Canadian anymore.

Not even the normal Albertan part that GG was.

GG?

My mom's grandma was born in Canada.

You are biologically Canadian on both sides???

No, just legally on Mom's.

GG's dad was Scottish and her mom was Minnesotan.

But he was supposedly a Mountie, so that has to count for something.

Points from this imaginary Canadian.

Weirdo.

So is this OK?

I guess.

Being friends with Francis is much easier.

Less . . . real.

I won't bother you at all about realness.

Clearly I'm rushing things.

But I'd rather have this than nothing at all.

Thanks, Francis.

I appreciate it.

Good.

Now I must go back to running errands.

CHUCK has some sort of thing for me to pick up to bring back to the office.

Ooh, maybe it's diamonds.

Not funny.

A LITTLE funny.

**8:48 p.m.**

Canada is a very strange place, Francis.

Have you FINALLY been studying?

What do you think the deal is with all dressed chips?

Think they're good?

I imagine they're overwhelming.

They might be good, though.

Did you know Canada wasn't even a fully sovereign nation until 1982?

???

Oh right.

The Commonwealth.

Right? Serves them right for snubbing their noses at us all those years ago.

Guess that better offer never came along.

Wait

Are YOU texting ME facts about Canada???

I guess.

I mean, we're not going to talk to each other tomorrow.

???

Well, I work, and you have baseball.

So we'll both be too busy.

Right

We won't see each other tomorrow.

Me still being Canadian and all.

Uh, I guess.

Mostly I figured you'd be busy.

Like a good imaginary internet friend.

You're being weird.

I'm fine.

Is everything okay at home?

Yep

We have way too much Chinese food and we're watching a movie.

Together time?

Cool Hand Luke

He just ate about a hundred eggs.

So disgusting.

Did you at least get vegetables?

Broccoli in the General Tso's?

Ew, did you actually eat it?

Yeah. What's wrong with General Tso's?

Nothing . . . I'll let you get back to your movie.

Oh, and have a good day tomorrow, Francis.

You too.

# TUESDAY, JULY 19
## 9:51 p.m.

I'm sorry

I can't do it.

What's wrong?

I can't go a whole day pretending not to talk to you.

I tried

I really did.

Okay.

Did you have something to say?

Yes

No

We won our game

I had a disgusting burger for lunch.

I got ice cream with my mother before the game . . .

Sounds super exciting.

I'm sorry.

This was ridiculous.

Whatever.

It's fine.

I gotta go.

It's plug-in.

Sorry

I'm TRYING to do better.

Don't change for my sake.

I didn't realize how fast this could be habit forming.

Good night, FRANCIS.

Good night, Haley.

I didn't NOT have anything to say last night.

What?

I had SOMETHING to say

But it was too late.

I didn't just want to say it.

It was fine.

They're engaged.

What?

Who?

Oh, wait. Your mom???

I realized dropping that on you seconds before plug-in would be unfair.

You should have told me.

I told you, that's my mom's soft spot. She would have been fine.

It's not that big of a deal.

It's kind of a big deal.

It is KIND OF a big deal.

Are you okay?

Other than the fact that CHUCK now calls me "Sport"?

Ew. Totally legit scare quotes.

I wouldn't be okay with that.

My father's not quite as OK as I am.

Oh, I bet not.

They were just together a couple of weeks ago and now she's engaged?

Maybe you should slip him some Tylenol.

That's not a terrible idea.

We can both suck on one and try not to ponder life.

It'll be better than this classic movie fest he seems to have planned for us.

Well, at least you're getting some culture out of it.

More like naps.

But what about your mom? Is she happy?

She seems to be

But

She's worried about me.

Isn't that like her job?

I guess that's why they split up earlier.

She doesn't want to marry him for real until after I graduate.

So next summer?

That's what she said.

OMG, you got ice cream yesterday!!!

I'm so self-centered.

I should have figured it was something like this.

Maybe I've dulled my own empathy receptors too much.

It's not like I actually told you anything had happened.

So did he get her a ring?

It's the size of a grapefruit.

Ew. I'd be petrified I'd lose it.

Or break it.

Nothing breaks diamonds.

Not true, one good whack of a hammer and it's dust.

I forgot I was talking to Geology Girl.

I am not Geology Girl!

Do you have a fan shirt yet?

This is what I get for sympathizing with you.

Sorry

I shouldn't tease you.

But you've got me smiling again.

Oh.

???

It's nothing.

Just . . .

???

No, nothing.

Never mind.

Forget I said anything, Francis.

Forgotten.

Okay, good.

Look, I should go.

Working on another project?

No, just something I need to take care of.

Thanks for listening.

Of course.

That's what friends are for.

Right.

### 7:42 p.m.

A proper Canadian maple leaf has
eleven points.

So what you're saying is that you're NOT
enjoying whatever classic movie your
father selected.

Diamonds Are Forever?

That would be a no.

UGH! No thank you.

So this mean you'll help me survive?

I consider it a solemn duty.

Excellent!

What are you doing?

Dramas. Mom and I are catching up for the week.

What does your father do while you watch your foreign television?

I don't know. Clean? Finish his dailies? Watch blacksmithing videos on YouTube?

The Canadian ones?

Oh, duh, those are Canadian!

So I guess I know some slang.

Canadian SLANG?

"Skookum" means "good" I think and "chooch" means "letting something work."

You were holding out on me?

Not on purpose.

I don't know if I can trust you anymore.

My father keeps asking me who I'm talking to.

What do you tell him?

I'm telling him Francis has to go tap a maple tree so I can focus on the epicness of his brilliant film selection.

You don't just have to keep making your parents happy, you know.

It's SO much easier when I do.

Yeah.

I get it.

Well, good night, Francis.

Good night, Francis.

# THURSDAY, JULY 21
## 9:28 a.m.

My mother just informed me we're having supper with CHUCK tonight.

> You're going to need your really nice shoes with the small laces.

No I won't.

She talked him into going to her favorite place.

> Really?

> Where's that?

This hole-in-the-wall Vietnamese restaurant.

She's obsessed with pho.

> She is?

Yes . . . but GOOD not fancy. His head is going to explode when he sees how cheap the menu is.

It's not Michelin star worthy.

> Is this on purpose?

I THINK she's trying to make me comfortable.

> Is she taking you for ice cream first?

How'd you guess?

> I mean if it works . . .

It MAY work.

I don't know anymore.

Twice in one week is too much?

She really wants me to like him.

Does she know you call him CHUCK?

Not yet.

Do you scream "I HATE YOU!" whenever you see him and then storm off to your room?

I'm quite polite to him I'll have you know.

How polite?

REALLY polite?

Like, your-grandma-at-a-charity-event polite?

Perhaps . . .

That's how she knows you don't like him.

I don't NOT like him.

I just don't want him to keep trying to impress me every five seconds.

Have you tried explaining that?

It seems to come out as more of a challenge.

How so?

He tries harder.

Well, maybe you could try a little?

I do try!!!

I mean, maybe pretend to be impressed?

Then I sound patronizing.

You don't.

There was a whole banana split three years ago about how intimidating I am to the men in her life.

Well, you ARE a Martin Munroe.

Captains of industry quiver at your footsteps.

People everywhere long for you wistfully in their dreams.

Whatever.

Okay, so, right, I get the patronizing.

Maybe just go along with it?

Be sullen or something.

Sullen?

Yes, pout.

Pretend for about five seconds to be a regular human teenager and not a future god among men or whatever.

Sullen.

You can't do it.

Oh no. I can

I'll think of something I really want and pretend it doesn't want anything to do with me.

Yes, good, that will work.

I'm glad you approve.

You're definitely getting it now.

I have to deliver some updated plans to a custom cabinet builder.

Isn't there email for that?

He's "folksy."

Hipsters.

Right?

**8:33 p.m.**

I'm still at supper

But he just offered to pay for my college education.

Quick

How do I tell him thanks but no thanks without reminding him of the fact that the family trust is worth more than his whole company????????

You suck at this.

I REALLY do.

Thank him kindly, but say that your grades are quite good and cost likely won't be a concern.

Imply scholarships.

Do you think that will work?

If that doesn't work, just stare at your shoes.

Shoes it is!!!

Lexi is over and she has a distinctly unfun plan for Friday Funday.

I'm sorry for interrupting.

No, you're fine.

Good luck!

Thanks.

**11:05 p.m.**

When you have a second . . .

Could I ask you some questions?

You know, as an internet friend.

If you aren't busy.

Why are you up???

Too much thinking.

Shouldn't you be in lockup?

Nah, my parents went out for once.

What are you up to?

Nothing.

Still doing the sullen thing?

I'm getting good at it

Had a lot of practice.

One evening?

Why aren't you sleeping?

Sullen

Remember?

Oh, I just thought . . .

???

Grandsons of a mogul whose family trust could buy and sell small nations slept like babes in the woods.

Can't sleep

Important stuff to do.

Such as?

Mogul's grandchildren are obligated to finish all their dailies and correct girls with wildly inaccurate ideas of what happens in Montreal at all hours.

Whatever, Francis.

You're smiling.

Am not.

But you had a question?

It's ridiculous.

I shouldn't ask.

Too late. Now I'm curious.

This is such a girl thing.

Like, I tried to talk to Lexi about it, but she just made it worse.

And I spent my whole day thinking.

Are you just full-on treating me like a girl???

This is harsh even for you.

Shut up.

You know what I mean.

Ask.

Okay, Francis.

Why aren't things easy when you like someone?

Why are you asking ME that?

I told you it was ridiculous.

Pretend I didn't ask.

Too late

Asked.

No, un-asked. Un-asked!

I was reading a really interesting article about female hormone replacements the other day.

NO, I'm answering the question!!!

I don't know why things are NEVER easy when you REALLY like someone.

You're useless.

Useless AND sullen for that very reason.

Why are you asking?

Part of the fight with Chloe.

???

I mean.

She's basically stolen my best friend. But SHE'S mad at ME about something that isn't even really a thing.

And I guess Sarah's crush might have actually become something and she still hasn't even told me about it.

I mean, I get why she wouldn't talk to me about it. I don't even know how to tell if I really like someone, let alone make it into something real.

You've gone out with a ton of girls. How do you even do that?

Just go up and say, "Hey, you're cute. Let's date"?

I wasn't aware I had gone out with nearly as many girls as I apparently have until I met you.

But it's not always that easy.

Why not?

There's a lot of other stuff in the way?

Like friends?

And history

Previous bad choices

Fear

Mostly fear.

What could you possibly be afraid of?

You'd be surprised.

I just hate not knowing what's up and what's down.

I hate that everyone seems to know what's really going on with me but me.

I hate that I'm stuck in this surreal situation.

Stuck in what?

. . .

I should probably go.

Are your parents back?

What?

No.

I just . . .

You should probably go?

Yeah.

Good night, Haley.

Good night, friend.

I forgot to ask last night: How did the rest of supper go?

I couldn't really help myself.

Uh-oh.

I MAY have mentioned Munroe Finance

And Munroe Capital.

You didn't.

There may have ALSO been a conversation about my aunt's latest boyfriend.

The documentary filmmaker?

No. She's back with the fashion designer.

Oh good.

I never liked that other dude.

His movies sucked.

He would have made things super tense at holidays.

Why?

His big money exposé on the banking industry is being submitted to Sundance.

Awkward!

Right?

So, basically, what you're saying is that you entirely failed at even managing sullen.

I told him he's got good taste.

You didn't.

In the pho place?

He may have turned red.

How mad is your mom?

WE decided I am spending the weekend at my father's

You're being punished by being sent back to the bachelor pad?

SHE didn't think SHE wanted to look at me right then.

Oh no.

Are you okay?

Not the worst thing that's happened to me this week.

Did something else happen?

What are YOU doing today?

Oh, right.

Friday Funday.

I told you. Lexi has a plan for Sarah and Chloe and me to "clear the air."

That sounds . . .

Fraught.

Exactly.

What about you?

Going out

Don't want to.

Sugar crash?

Something like that.

Well, good luck rallying.

Good luck with whatever Lexi has in store.

**5:18 p.m.**

Lexi's plan . . .

It isn't an Escape Room . . . is it?

Yeah. Where'd you hear that?

Uhm

Well

See you there?

NO!

Yes.

Just you?????

Me

Gabe

Wade

ll

Jack

She said she had a full room. I figured it was her art friends.

ll decided he REALLY needs out of a locked room.

I really need out of this.

You want out?

I'm literally trapped in Lexi's mom's car this second.

We're in a drive-thru.

There's no getting out.

It won't be THAT bad.

I can't believe she'd do this to me.

To us.

I thought she wanted to fix whatever was going on with Sarah and Chloe.

Breathe.

We'll be locked in a room for an hour.

There will be puzzles!

No wonder Lexi's been smiling like that.

Oh god. Why me?

Are you worried Chloe will say something in front of everyone?

Just . . . do me a favor.

Pretend you don't know me.

If you can keep your cousin away . . .

No, won't matter.

Do you need me to get out of this?

NO!

I need you there.

Promise me.

???

When Chloe's around, make sure NO ONE talks to me.

Not a single Martin will talk to you around Chloe

I promise.

And Jack too.

You know, for safety.

OK . . .

Trust me.

If we don't, the murder we'll be solving will be mine.

I don't get why you're doing this.

Lexi begged.

Now I know why . . .

I've gotta drive

Will you be all right?

Trying to remember how to breathe.

**7:52 p.m.**

I swear we're going to need a real necromancer if anyone expects both of us to make it out of here alive.

Where are you?

Chloe's on my very last nerve.

Why does she think she's the boss?

She's not the boss.

We're ALL in the same advanced classes.

She's not freaking smarter than us.

Of course she's not.

No one's even listening to her except you

It's fine

If she keeps bossing me around, I may not be able to handle it.

Seriously where are you?

I'm under the tilter . . .

The what?

The round table in the corner.

The one with the lace on it?

You're hiding under a table texting me?

"Hiding" is a strong word . . .

You're hiding from her!

I'm not hiding from her.

I'm avoiding her.

There's a difference.

You don't have to hide from her.

Get out here and let's solve the puzzle so she knows she's not the smartest one here.

I am solving the puzzle.

I'm not hiding. I told you.

This is the table they use to commune with the specters.

The what?

Ghosts of the dead nobility.

When the specter manifests, where do you think that will happen?

You found a clue?

Of course I did!

It's a cipher.

So bring it out so we all can see.

I'd rather hide . . .

You're going to get eaten by a ghost.

Specters consume other nobles, not people.

Then why do we care if it appears?

Because they DO turn them into mindless drones. Have you not read ANY of the books???

Why would I have read these books?

Useless!!!

Utterly.

But let me have a chance at that cipher
and we'll see if I stay that way.

Oh fine.

**8:59 p.m.**

That wasn't so bad.

We failed the room.

But we didn't use a hint!

Chloe screamed at me.

And then that clown screamed at her.

...

You promised you'd keep him away.

She brought this on herself.

We could have vanquished the specter
so easily, but everything imploded.

This was from one of your kissing books,
wasn't it?

A poor approximation AT BEST.

You don't have to win them all.

I could have won if you three were home
playing 3v3 instead.

But I'm not

I'm here

And since we're here we should talk.

You think?

Where are you?

I'll find you.

No, I think I see you . . .

Be right there.

Wait

Give me a second.

**9:11 p.m.**

Where are you?

**9:28 p.m.**

Are you still here?

**10:15 p.m.**

Did you make it home OK?

Where did you end up?

**11:19 p.m.**

Are you there?

Why aren't you answering?

Did something happen???

Mr. Munroe?

Yes

Is there a reason you're saved under "Francis the Canadian"?

A joke?

I believe you know the rules.

I apologize, Mrs. Hancock.

I hope I didn't wake you.

No, I've been awake since Haley's declared quite loudly the only Martin she has any interest in speaking to is Dr. King because "he's not a liar."

So I cannot say I'm surprised you're messaging this late.

Was this your doing?

I'm afraid it must be.

Haley will speak to you in the morning when she has found her words again.

Yes, ma'am. I'm very sorry for disturbing you.

## SATURDAY, JULY 23
### 10:14 a.m.

I don't want to talk to you.

Whatever happened I'm sorry.

Don't bother me.

Don't bother my mom.

Don't be nice to her.

Just . . .

Don't.

What happened?

I don't talk to liars.

. . .

That's all you have to say?

???

How did I figure it out?

Yeah

I saw you.

Then Chloe connected all the dots about Wade's party.

I can't believe I trusted you.

I told you I'm still me no matter what.

It was right in front of my face this whole time.

I'm sorry.

You should be.

I don't know why I thought this was real.

I don't know what I thought.

Please don't hate me.

I don't know if I can.

You played me.

It's not like that!!!

It is.

You . . .

UGH.

Don't talk to me.

I'm really sorry, Haley.

Hurting you was the last thing I ever wanted.

Yeah . . . well . . . you're really good at it.

I can't believe I thought this was real.

Were you ever going to tell me?

I didn't know how.

Are you there?

If you're there answer me.

You can hate me again when I'm done.

After the Escape Room what exactly did you see that freaked you out???

Shouldn't you be with your girlfriend?

Was that what you saw?

I believe I made it clear I don't want to talk to you.

Answer me

Please

Please?

Yes, I saw you two together, all right?

I mean, I figured out your big secret. Big deal. Who cares? You've just been lying for weeks.

By together you mean . . .

Kissing. Okay?

I SAW YOU AND SARAH KISSING.

Is that what you wanted to hear?

That I caught you?

So when you said you saw me

When you freaked out

It was because you thought you saw Sarah kissing me?

OMG, when you put it that way, I sound super jealous.

I swear it wasn't like that. I'm only mad that you lied to me, okay?

Let me get this straight

I . . . Martin Nathaniel Munroe II . . . am a liar because I kissed Sarah Eastman on Friday night?

Why do you keep saying it?

Because

Augh

I hate my life

Why?

Because I caught you?

What's wrong with that?

Nothing

Everything

I've got to go

We're at the restaurant

But we HAVE to talk later.

So you can lie to me some more?

**5:23 p.m.**

I knew there was a complication

I didn't think it had gotten THIS complicated.

I hear the relationship or whatever it is was made official at church this morning.

In the most dramatic way possible.

I shouldn't pry.

I wish you would.

No, I don't want to know what anyone has to say about Sarah and any of the Munroes dating ever again.

You're a liar and that clown didn't even come into the gas station this whole week.

After Friday it's clear even he really wants nothing to do with me.

The maniac burrito clown is a fool who didn't think he deserved burritos this week.

Is he okay?

He's been dealing with some stuff.

I'm trying to give you credit for at least trying to tell me at Wade's party.

This means I still have to talk to you.

What? Why?

Everything's out in the open now.

Not even remotely.

Oh.

Ohhhh.

Wait.

You WERE going to tell me, right?

???

About you and Sarah.

Or were you just going to let me find out?

Or is Chloe right? Are you Munroes just playing with me???

What we need to talk about has nothing to do with Sarah AT ALL.

But regardless of Chloe's unnecessary drama this is STILL not something I can do on the phone.

So you weren't going to tell me you were dating?

Hasn't this been bad enough?

Does she even know we've been talking?

STOP.

Not everything in the entire world is about them.

You're dating my best friend but talking to me ALL the time!!!!!

How is this not about that?

Please

Just stop.

We need to REALLY talk.

Can I come over now?

No. My parents have people over.

Tomorrow?

I'm babysitting tomorrow.

Lunch Tuesday???

I work Tuesday.

Exactly

I'll come in on my lunch.

I thought this wasn't something to hash out over burritos.

This isn't what you think

Not even a tiny bit what you think

Please don't avoid me.

I have to go . . . my parents want me to play a game with them.

Now?

They want to do an emperor game in Magic but need six players.

Please don't freak out when you see me.

You don't get to tell me what to do.

This is all going to be OK.

I can fix this.

You're not freaking out about tomorrow

Right?

I'm not done being mad at you if that's what you're asking.

I promise I'm going to explain.

That's fine, but I can't talk about it now.

Are you that mad?

I'm in a tense negotiation.

???

My cousin refuses to eat his favorite food.

My only advice for cousins right now involves extreme violence.

Are you fighting with him?

What's happening? I heard you guys were arguing after church. Is he okay?

Get back to your negotiations.

We'll talk tomorrow.

Don't be too rough on him if he's really having a bad time.

My cousin doesn't even know what a bad time looks like yet.

## 9:45 p.m.

Are you still working tomorrow?

On the schedule.

And you're healthy
Not getting a summer cold?

Considering it.

You NEED to see me
I need to see you
We need to see each other.

Look, I gotta go.

I know.
Just . . .

Good night, Francis.

No.
No more Francis.

# TUESDAY, JULY 26
## 11:45 a.m.

I'm going to be a little late.

I've gotta pick up one last thing.

## 7:05 p.m.

If coming in with Sarah is the message, I got it loud and clear.

In fact, I figured out something today that I hadn't realized.

Our relationship kinda sucks.

No, that's not true. Texting you is awesome. Too awesome. More awesome than it should be.

But in real life, you're a bit too good at this pretending thing.

I don't think I can do it anymore.

None of this. Not pretending. Not talking to you. Not even our conversations being awesome.

In fact, the being awesome is the worst part.

You know, I got so confused I thought maybe you were going to tell me you liked me at Wade's party?

No. I wanted you to like me because it would be easier.

You two . . . with your confusing names and all your mixed messages . . .

You would be easier.

You got me.

But I don't know how you can talk to me this much and start dating my friend.

I don't know how I can pretend to your faces that I'm happy for you.

I don't know why I thought this would be different.

Chloe was right. That night at Wade's party.

I was deluding myself to think either of you would ever pick me.

I'm just a fun internet friend. That's all I ever am. All I'll be to anyone.

Then . . . on Friday. That look in your eye.

It was like I didn't even exist.

Your freaking COUSIN was nicer to me than you.

In fact, he's been way nicer to me all summer than you have even once in person.

You both got me so mixed up . . .

I mean, I get it, you're going through some stuff. Your family situation sucks, but that's not an excuse.

None of this is an excuse.

And that's the thing. I've been making excuses for both of you all along.

You, in the store, holding her hand. That's when I figured out that this is imaginary.

You are imaginary. I made you up. You might as well really be Francis.

No one's that good of an actor.

So I'm out. I'm done.

Whatever this is . . . it's finished.

I can't believe I ever thought you were the good one.

Chloe was right. Everything's a game to you two.

I can't believe I lost.

**9:28 p.m.**

I can't believe you're not even good enough to answer me.

## WEDNESDAY, JULY 27
### 10:04 a.m.

Really?

You haven't even responded?

I really HAVE been fooling myself.

Look, I'm not trying to talk about you. I just wanted to know if your cousin is all right.

Lexi said he'd had some sort of accident at work.

And that's when I realized . . . despite having had him over to lunch and hanging out at the con with him, I have no freaking idea what his phone number is.

If you'd at least be kind enough to let me know if he's okay, or how to contact him, or anything, I'd appreciate it.

You can manage at least that much can't you?

### 4:58 p.m.

Okay, this is ridiculous.

You should at least be off work now.

No, you should at least be mature enough to answer a simple request.

Man, I'm an idiot.

## THURSDAY, JULY 28
### 6:15 p.m.

least you could do is come visit your boy

### 7:03 p.m.

Who is this?

you know who it is

Jack?

yeah dingbat

Why are you on Martin's phone?

because he cant be

hes sleeping right now

And again I ask . . .

they gave him some serious drugs

he's not all there but they're finally letting him have visitors

not that he's up for anything more than whining about you

and you dont even have the courtesy to come check on him

What are you talking about?

you have to have heard about M's accident by now

I heard he was in the hospital.

I've been trying to get his contact information for days.

well this is his phone how else would you expect to contact him dingbat

Stop calling me that!

You know how much I hate it!

I mean, you have to know how much girls would hate it.

i know its you H

Crap.

CRAP!

What's going on?

What happened?

he was making some sort of delivery and there was an accident

the dude his moms seeing wanted to show him a real construction site and he tripped in a hole and bonked his head

lucky he was wearing a hard hat

Oh crap. He's okay?

Why is he on drugs?

the super brain got shaken up and he jacked up his shoulder

I'm so confused.

I thought it was the other one who was hurt?

you're confused about a great number of things

this is why youre our dingbat

Shut up and explain it to me, then.

cant both shut up and explain

How could both of them have accidents at the same time?

you still dont get it

do you

I really don't.

i figured this was a bro code thing and thats why he didnt seal the deal

but you think hes II

Could you use English for once in your life?

I am on M's phone

That doesn't help.

then you tell me

how do you tell the munroes apart

I don't.

clearly

you both think youre so smart

I am just about done with this conversation.

not if you know whats good for you

I am gonna try one more time.

You're saying that only one of the Martins had an accident?

yup

The Martin who had an accident is also the owner of this phone?

yup

And the accident that the owner of this phone had was at his future stepdad's construction company?

yup

Where is Sarah?

probably out sucking JJ's face somewhere

Not at the hospital?

there may be light at the end of this tunnel

nope

Because she's not dating the Martin who owns this phone?

not since she made a giant scene behind the craft cabin and threw his leather cuff in his face because she was jealous of all the time he was spending with his cabinmates

Wait, what?

come on everyone knows that

I thought he cheated on her.

thats because you'll believe anything she says dingbat

I am so confused.

clearly

look

i get you may be dingy but the boy is hurting and you may be the only thing that can help

so im giving you permission to date him even tho it will break my heart into a thousand pieces

I need a minute.

I just . . .

Give me a minute.

dont take too long

How are you even on his phone?

i have known M since he was in diapers

known him longer than II has

you think i dont know his secret code

You seem to know a lot more than I ever gave you credit for.

this happens

look

sorry for messing with you at the game

i was still a little pissed and didnt know you were that slow

Neither of us is slow.

We get better grades than you with our eyes closed.

grades

like that even matters when you cant see whats going on right in front of your face

I . . .

Just . . .

Shut up, JACKSON!!!

theres my dingbat

STOP CALLING ME THAT!

stop being one and i will

## FRIDAY, JULY 29
### 3:15 p.m.

R U my Martin's friend Haley?

Uhm, I mean, I think so.

U think U are Haley?

No, I'm definitely Haley.

I don't get U kids these days

This is his mother

Oh, hello. I'm sorry. Yes. I'm Haley.

My martin wanted me to tell U he's gng to be all right.

He says he's sorry for missing UR appointment and worries you may be freaking out

Those are his words not mine

He said put freaking in quotes but I don't knw how

That sounds like the Martin I know.

He says U R probly confused

Extraordinarily.

I am so mad at Charles for letting him near the site

But my Martin will be released 2morrow

He will contact U then

Thank you.

Is there a message for him?

Just that I look forward to hearing his side of all this when he feels better.

U R so good with this tiny keyboard

I will tell him

And thank you for letting me know he's okay.

U R welcome

R U the Haley we met at church?

Oh, well, yeah. I'm that Haley.

Good

# SATURDAY, JULY 30
## 7:28 p.m.

Look. I can explain everything.

Who is this?

Martin Nathaniel Munroe II

Which one?

...

The one that's in love with you.

I don't know which one that is.

You do

You have to

This is the Martin who tells you everything

Who introduced you to his family the first chance he got

Who binged every episode of Orphan Black just to talk to you about Felix and Helena.

This is the Martin who takes acetaminophen when he's worried he'll end up ruining this relationship the way his father ruins his

The Martin who lied to me.

No.

OK yes.

A lot.

I was afraid.

It feels like everything you've ever said was a lie.

I didn't know I was lying at first

Then I did

But it didn't seem like that big of a deal

And then it was too late.

I knew you would hate me the second you found out

You would have had reason to.

What makes you think I don't?

The fact that you're worried about me.

Yeah. I am worried. Are you okay?

What really happened?

CHUCK.

Charles

Whatever.

His site was my last stop before I was supposed to meet you.

So you never actually came on Tuesday.

I don't even know why II and Sarah were there.

I do . . . Sarah was showing him off.

She told everyone at church, then she had to show me. After everyone else, she finally told me.

That was cold.

Yeah. Well, we had a fight of our own.

She had the nerve to say that Chloe said I'd be like this and that's why she didn't tell me.

I'm done with them. I just can't anymore.

Finally

But that's not important

THEY'RE not important.

You were really going to tell me yourself?

Twice

The first time at Wade's party.

And I screwed it up.

YOU didn't.

I did.

I let Chloe get to me.

Let her convince me . . .

???

She said I deserved it if I actually believed you would ever be interested in me.

She said that?

She'd been hearing things. Figured out Lexi's not-so-subtle jokes.

She wanted to make sure I knew my place and we wouldn't end up together.

With who?

You . . .

The burrito clown.

Oh no, I called you a clown.

You wouldn't be you if you didn't.

Usually I'm better at judging people.

You're maybe 50/50.

But . . .

Okay, fine, about 50/50.

But not on the big stuff.

No . . . you're worse with the big stuff.

Clearly.

But I already know how I got hurt.

Can you please finish telling me how you got hurt?

I was trying to get out of there to meet you but Charles insisted on showing me the site.

UGH. So he was showing off?

When is he not???

Even tho I was in a hurry all I could hear was you saying I should make an effort.

So I put on a stupid hard hat and let him show me around.

I was TRYING

I was just a little distracted.

Because you were late.

Someone shouted a heads-up and I looked up.

Whatever it was wasn't anywhere near me

I tripped and landed in a big hole.

Oh no.

Are you all right?

Concussion

Sprained shoulder.

Charles was amazing. Totally in control the whole time.

He talked to me and got them to call the ambulance. He even kept my mother calm at the hospital.

It's not as bad as it could be

Worse than when I took a fall skiing.

That bad.

Are you sure you're okay to type?

It was my other arm

My typing thumb is fine.

That's not what I mean.

You should be resting.

I "rested" for three whole days

I NEED to be doing this now.

You need to be sleeping. I'm fine. I heard everything.

. . . You didn't read all the nonsense I wrote, did you?

And your conversation with Jack.

I'm definitely upgrading to the facial recognition now.

He'll probably figure that out too.

He may not be bright, but he's smarter than I thought.

Way better than 50/50 with us.

Tell me about it.

What you said on Tuesday

I made assumptions again.

Not that.

I was just mad.

I'm glad you were mad

I'm also glad you were ready to cut me off.

Even more glad you told Sarah and Chloe off.

And just so you know

If Jack hadn't told you . . . I wouldn't have made you wait.

What?

Why?

You gave me courage.

Me yelling at you?

You said you liked me

That helped.

I was trying to hurt you with that.

No

You said you liked ME

Not II.

I said I thought I liked the person I was talking to and his cousin at the same time.

Me.

I can't even tell if you're real.

Nothing is more real than who I am right now.

Since when have you guys been going by M and II?

Since he moved to town so . . . preschool.

Really?

You never noticed?

I never really cared.

We were beneath your dignity?

Outside my sphere of influence.

You dated my best friend.

Not willingly.

I dated YOUR best friend.

When you guys were away at summer camp.

. . .

Speaking of . . . why didn't you correct me on that?

It didn't matter.

Nothing about her mattered.

That whole relationship would have been as pointless as all the others except she helped me realize the boy in sixth grade wasn't a fluke

You liked one of your cabinmates . . .

I haven't always been as good at keeping secrets as I am now.

I don't know about that.

You didn't want to see the truth.

I didn't know there was a truth to see.

I should have told you

After Paris

I should have confessed.

That's also true.

But . . .

???

You weren't wrong.

At the beginning of the summer, I definitely would have freaked out on you.

I did.

I have been.

When not freaking out about you getting hurt.

You still can't forgive me.

I didn't say that.

But I realized that the Martins I thought I knew at the beginning of the summer aren't the Martins I know now.

???

Just . . . all of it.

Talking to you.

Him dating Sarah.

Chloe making things complicated when they didn't need to be.

. . . It's all not what I thought.

And?

Well, so maybe you didn't lie to me during our first conversation.

???

I asked which Martin I was talking to.

I DID say I was the good one

You did.

You'll forgive me?

I'm still working on that.

It's time for me to take some acetaminophen mixed with something in the opiate family.

Are you in a lot of pain?

SO MUCH. But the existential dread isn't helping.

I'm sorry.

It's a bit better now

I won't need it to help with my heartache.

Right?

I've created a monster.

You love it.

We'll see.

Please take care of yourself.

I just want to point out one thing

What's that?

It wasn't a car accident.

Huh?

You were always worried I'd have a car accident.

I didn't.

No, you only fell in a hole. You're lucky you didn't land on rebar.

I didn't do that either.

You have to pay attention or you'll miss stuff.

Pot

Kettle is on the phone

It would like to discuss color options with you.

Har, har.

This is me BEFORE drugs.

Go rest.

Please don't hate me.

After that joke I'm considering it.

Good night, Haley.

Good night, M.

# SUNDAY, JULY 31
## 11:15 a.m.

How are you doing?

You're probably in church, ignore that.

You get to skip church when you're on drugs.

Get to, or just choose not to go?

In my family it's GET to.

Tho that doesn't stop some of them.

Oh, right. I saw your aunt's meme.

That was blown way out of proportion.

She fell out of a limousine.

She just put her foot down wrong.

Well, I guess I'm not one to judge.

This is NOT what you wanted to talk about.

No, I just wanted to see how you're doing.

That depends.

On?

How are you doing?

Still need to think.

How much time do you need?

That's what I wanted to talk to you about.

I'm going away, remember?

The con

Where is it?

Indiana.

Four days of gaming.

But we're leaving early.

???

Mom's birthday. We're going to celebrate on our way.

What's on your way???

She wants to go to H Mart and Shedd Aquarium.

H Mart?

It's a giant Korean grocery store.

What's she getting there?

Snacks mostly, but also some stuff for the kitchen.

Dad really wants some dolsot bowls for home.

Dolsot???

Giant stone bowls you heat up on the stove and serve crispy rice in.

That's . . .

Awesome?

I can see how that might work.

I know. We like awesome stuff.

When are you back?

Super late next Sunday.

Will you talk to me then?

I'll consider it if you get yourself better.

Do you promise to think about what I said?

I swear. I won't do anything but.

And look at penguins.

How'd you know about Pororo?

At the aquarium?

Oh, right they'll have penguins there too.

Should I be jealous of this named penguin???

No. Jealousy is not on the table.

I'll do my best.

Just be careful.

I should be telling you that.

I'm going to be in bed most of the time

Especially if my mother has any say.

Which she totally does.

Listen to your mother.

Like when she says I should invite that "sweet Haley girl" over???

We'll see about that part.

We're having dinner with Charles tonight anyway.

Charles?

I MAY actually be mature enough to reconsider hating someone when they save my life.

That does seem quite grown-up of you.

I blame you.

Just not for you being late. That was all you.

I'd kick myself if everything didn't still hurt.

But I really mean it. Take care of yourself while I'm gone.

You too.

And, Haley

Yeah?

I'll miss you.

## THURSDAY, AUGUST 4
### 9:18 p.m.

> I still have no service.

> Chicago was fun.

> Penguins were cute.

> I saw three Deadpools today and had to tell you.

> Gotta go!

Glad you're having fun.

## FRIDAY, AUGUST 5
### 10:20 p.m.

Four more Deadpools and even a Nux.

I may actually have a celebrity crush on War Boys!!!

But no. I just remembered how they treat women, so . . . never mind.

Oh, and there was a young Professor X too. The cool wheels and everything.

Just had to tell you.

You're not running off with any of them???

# SATURDAY, AUGUST 6
## 8:25 p.m.

I'm so tired I can't move

There was a Green Lantern today.

I wasn't sure if you'd want to know or not.

I want to know everything.

## MONDAY, AUGUST 8
### 10:35 a.m.

Hey, stranger.

### 12:05 p.m.

Is this really you or another celebrity crush cosplay update?

Really me. We got in a little earlier than planned, so I didn't need to sleep all day.

How did it go?

It was fun. Played a bunch of new games. Saw assorted penguins, Deadpools, and a bunch of X-Men.

You didn't run off with any?

I'm not you. I came back like I said I would.

Though there was discussion about kidnapping a War Boy and making him drive us all the way back.

That seems . . .

Excessive.

So was an eleven-hour drive.

But it was good.

Lexi called me.

On the phone?

With her voice?

Yeah, I swear she was born twenty years too late.

But she helped me see things in a different kind of way.

???

She said she had suspicions about us all summer.

She said she's on my side whatever goes down.

AGAINST Chloe?

Oh yeah. I think she hates her more than I do.

That loudmouth Jack told someone who told someone who told Dylan.

Chloe knows too.

I guess she came looking for me.

But you were gone.

Yeah.

Not that it matters.

You're not worried about what Chloe will think?

Nope.

I'm done with that.

As Lexi said, it's Sarah's turn to start acting like she's our friend.

I like Lexi.

Lexi is smart.

Listen to Lexi.

Yeah. Lexi was crying because she thought I thought she wouldn't be there for me.

She's mad she had to hear about all this third hand. Like she did with Sarah and II.

Chloe convinced Lexi that Sarah and I were done with her because of all that stuff with Dylan. So now I'm at war with Chloe and all of Chloe-kind.

But I told Lexi the truth.

What's that?

That I wasn't sure what was real.

And . . . that I really don't want to do any more Hump Day quizzes.

Her response?

That she has been shipping you and me since the barbecue.

That if I'd told her . . . she'd have helped.

That I have a permanent quiz exemption so long as I promise to talk to her on a regular basis.

That sounds manageable.

Yeah, I think I'll have plenty to talk to her about . . .

When I told her why I really hated the quizzes, she showed me a different quiz.

According to that I'm not weird . . .

I'm demisexual.

Where'd she find that?

I don't know. I guess she's been doing research for the quizzes and came across some stuff that she thought people needed to see.

She wasn't being sketchy. She was trying to help in her own Lexi way.

But whatever.

Are you back at work already?

I am

My mother has officially turned it into a desk job now, but she's keeping me busy.

You still down a limb?

I've got a brace

I can't carry phyllosilicates around.

I CAN file and tape up receipts.

Sounds exciting.

You have no idea.

Dylan's mystery source is not the only one who talked to Jack while you were gone.

You always talk to Jack.

I mean I REALLY talked to him.

Not in the playing-Xbox kind of way?

Well . . . we played PS4 WHILE we talked.

Did he go all bro on you?

It wasn't touchy feely but it was good to ACTUALLY talk.

Even if you decide to hate me I'll have at least figured out how real friends talk.

We even managed to talk about you a little.

You didn't.

A little.

We had stuff to clear up.

Ugh.

I guess I'm really not as good at hiding things from him as I thought.

I don't know if anyone is.

He's kinda creepy now.

He's observant

That's why he knew to like you first

He even saw all this before I did.

All what?

Us

How we fit

The mess I was making

He suspected I was texting you after he gave me your number.

In MAY?!?

He confirmed it that day you came to church

It pissed him off . . . which is why he broke into my phone

But we were so pitiful (his words) he decided to help.

You mean the baseball game was him trying to help?

In his messed-up-Jack kind of way.

Tell him not to help again!

I'm glad he did.

You know I wouldn't completely hate you.

You did before.

Well, yeah, but I didn't know you then.

You weren't real.

Now I'm real?

A little too real.

Are you freaked out?

Never not.

Look, can we meet?

I'm working now.

After work?

Where?

My house?

You know where that is.

You've been here.

You've made a decision?

Yeah. But as you said, it's an in-person thing.

Cool.

Drive carefully, okay?

Of course.

I wouldn't miss this for the world.

I mean it.

I swear I'll be hyper vigilant.

Maybe you should get a Lyft.

My mother has cleared me to drive just not for work.

You can too.

Okay, fine. If your mom says so.

So I'll talk to you after work, I guess.

Definitely.

**8:14 p.m.**

What are you doing???

I'm reading this super interesting article on closed time-like curves in BTZ black holes.

I see . . .

Why?

I enjoyed dinner with your family and that was a really cool game we played

But . . .

But?

Are you sure? That stuff you said earlier?

What about it?

You're ready for us to be a thing?

Well . . .

Yeah.

Why?

Then would you PLEASE put your phone down?

What? Why?

I'd very much like to kiss you now.

# ACKNOWLEDGMENTS

A book is never just a book, it's all the stories that came before and every experience that brought those words to that page. I don't have room to acknowledge every experience that brought me to this point, so here's a sampling:

First of all, thank you to my lovely agent, Bridget Smith, who not only saw Haley for who she was but has been helping me through my adventures in publishing even before she knew who I was. To my brilliant editor, Jody Corbett, who loves these two nerds nearly as much as I do and was willing to go to battle over commas. And to everyone at Scholastic Press who has gone above and beyond for my strange little book, especially Baily Crawford for making it so very pretty; Josh Berlowitz for fitting it into a book-shaped thing; and Rachel Feld, Julia Eisler, Elisabeth Ferrari, and the amazing sales teams for getting so very many people excited.

Thank you, Beth Phelan, for creating #DVpit, a space where writers can share their stories, even when the world pushes the dream further away.

I wouldn't be here without my writer gang: Adib Khorram, who read everything, even the pizza party. Kosoko Jackson, who shared EVERY LITTLE up and down along the way. Kaitlyn Sage Patterson, who believed in this story before I did. Michelle Hulse, who shared her brave publishing adventures. And Mary, who knows the difference between typhoid and typhus (and pushed me to write Haley's story authentically). Cabin 81, thank you for being there when I needed you most; I wish you all the best wherever your path may lead. And special shout-out to everyone from the AmberMUSH days who drilled voice into me and made grammar and punctuation cool.

And all my friends who supported me: Sarah Moeller over many lunches, Joel Roth and Adana Washington over many chats, and Peter and Robbie over many years.

I could not possibly have written this book without my day jobs. aBt made technology easy—thank you, Doug, for always expecting me to accomplish the impossible and giving me at least a day to do it. The Bridge for Youth gave me a place to connect with my community; thank you, Sue and Alisha, for being there every step of the way. And thank you, Fran, for being the one true Francis.

Matt, thank you for surviving all of everything with me. Michael, thank you for bringing my life joy. Monica, thank you for making all my dreams seem reachable. Thank you for being my family.

# ABOUT THE AUTHOR

Lana Wood Johnson was born and raised in Iowa in the time before the internet but has spent the rest of her life making up for that. After years working in wireless communication for companies of all sizes, she now works doing the same for a local youth shelter. Lana lives in Minnesota with her husband and their English bulldog.